BETWEEN EMBERS

(LOST KINGS MC #5.5)

AUTUMN JONES LAKE

A COMPANION TO WHITE HEAT

COPYRIGHT

Between Embers
Lost Kings MC #5.5
A companion to White Heat
Copyright 2016 Autumn Jones Lake
All Rights Reserved
Digital ISBN # 978-1-943950-07-2
Paperback ISBN #978-1-943950-08-9
Edited by PREMA
Cover Photo: Dollar Photo Club
Cover Design: AJ Lake

ABOUT BETWEEN EMBERS

If you were wondering what some of the other LOKI men were up to during Rock and Hope's wedding...this is your chance to find out.

Between Embers (Lost Kings MC #5.5) is a collection of three short stories. This is intended to be a companion to *White Heat (Lost Kings MC #5)*. If you do not enjoy reading similar scenes from a different character's point of view, then please skip this. If you like to complain that short stories are *too short*, this is not the book for you.

On the other hand, if you were curious about what Teller was doing the morning of the wedding. What Murphy and Heidi talked about when she arrived at the clubhouse, or how Z and Lilly spent the night, I think you'll enjoy *Between Embers*.

ACKNOWLEDGMENTS

I'm lucky to have a lot of supportive and encouraging people in my life. This seems like a good place to express my appreciation.

Mr. Lake, thanks for always being in my corner.

Thank you once again to Shelly, Angi, Clarisse, Tamra, Elizabeth, Amanda, Robin, and Iveta for your feedback. Than you to Andrea, Tanya, and Elizabeth for reviewing these short stories on short notice.

Thank you to my crit partners, who encouraged me to go ahead when I was ready to give up.

Thank you to my editor, Vanessa for giving me this idea.

Most of all, thank you to my wonderful readers who keep pushing and inspiring me every day.

FOREWORD

If you've purchased *Between Embers* and are now reading this, I'll assume you're more than just a casual fan of the series. These short stories are for you. Let me share with you how *Between Embers* came to be.

While we were in the process of editing *White Heat*, my editor made a comment about how it seemed an awful lot was going on with the other guys and she wanted to know what they were up to during the wedding. Of course, in my head, I knew exactly what everyone was up to. My secondary characters don't *know* they're secondary characters. However, it was impossible to show their activities through Rock and Hope's point-of-views, or even Wrath and Trinity's and it would have been extraneous in a book that was ready approach 125,000 words.

But the idea wouldn't go away!

I'd been planning to do another book of short stories like *Three Kings, One Night* for a while now. I really love those stories—not everyone does because they're "too short" (to which I always think which part of **short stories** was misleading?) To me they're important to the series to give background on some of the characters who at the time when I published them, hadn't been featured yet. I have referred back to them on several occasions.

Anyway, I've wanted to do another collection similar to *Three Kings* for a while and just haven't been able to fit it in my writing schedule. My plan was to add *Infatuated*, the story featuring Z and Lilly that was included in the *Pink: Hot & Sexy Anthology*, since that is no longer available, one of Rock and Hope finally using their basement, and one other couple.

Except, I've been so caught up in Murphy's world, toiling away at *More Than Miles (Lost Kings MC #6)* and one or two other projects, that this was pushed aside.

The damn idea for "between the wedding" stories wouldn't go away, though!

Then I came up with—what I thought—was a killer title "Between the Embers" (then I whittled it down to *Between Embers* so it had two words like *White Heat*, since it's a companion piece to *White Heat*) while sitting in a CR-RWA workshop (I get some of my best ideas at my CR-RWA chapter meetings—thanks guys!) Once I figure out a title, I get so excited, I'm committed to the project, but damn that Murphy didn't make things easy on me!

As is my process, I had bits and pieces of each story written out. A few things that happen in *Between Embers* are critical (in my head) to future books, but this series is my baby, so naturally I think everything is critical.

There it is. *Between Embers* is intended to be a fun collection of stories to go along with *White Heat*. If you haven't read it yet, these stories won't make a lot of sense to you.

If you're still reading—thank you! I hope you enjoy these little "between the scenes" glimpses into the world of the Lost Kings MC.

TIMELINE

Between Embers contains chunks of time that were not seen in *White Heat.* Each story covers the same time period. Some events you *did* see in *White Heat* and you'll now see them here through a different character's eyes.

Teller's story starts early the morning of the wedding and ends when he goes to bed. Murphy's story also starts early in the morning and ends after the reception. Z's story starts before the wedding and ends the following morning.

TELLER

THE DAY HASN'T EVEN STARTED, and I'm exhausted. I'm up at this hour so I can run home and pick up Heidi. I'm not expecting to run into the bride in the kitchen.

"Oh, Teller. You startled me."

I run my gaze from her shiny robe, shorts, over her bare legs, and down to her fluffy slippers. "What are you doing in here?" My voice comes out harsher than I mean it to, so I force a smile.

Hope sets a carton of milk down on the counter. "I don't know. I was going to eat breakfast, but I'm too nervous."

"As long as you're not plannin' a getaway." I was trying to be funny, but I just sound like an overbearing jerk.

She ignores me and pulls a loaf of bread out of the fridge, popping two slices in the toaster. "Do you want anything?"

"Coffee."

"You're on your own there. Every time I try to make coffee, it tastes like burned beans."

"Trinity's the one who knows how to make the coffee."

She chuckles softly. "Yup."

"So, you happy you'll be out of the clubhouse after tonight?" Again, I sound more like a cop interrogating her rather than the respectful way I should talk to my president's ol' lady and I'm not sure why.

"I don't think the house is ready for us yet."

Prez said it would be ready tonight. He *also* said it was a surprise. I'm not sure why it bothers me that they're moving out. It's none of my business. "No. You know what I mean."

"It will be nice to be alone with my husband." Her lips curve into a dreamy smile. "But I'll probably miss you guys. It's impossible to be lonely here."

Her words sock me in the gut, but I cover it up with a joke. "Come on, you'll be happy to get away from all us dirty horndogs."

"Well, I've definitely seen my share of things that can't be unseen." She fake shivers and I can't help laughing.

"You're so calm. I remember when he married Carla, she was a maniac. Screaming and yelling at everyone."

Her jaw drops and her cheeks redden.

"Shit. I'm sorry. That was rude to—"

"It's fine, Teller." She shrugs and tosses her hair back. "It's not like I don't know he was married before."

She grabs her toast, smearing butter all over it, then tossing the knife in the sink. "You must have been young then."

"Fifteen? Sixteen? I don't really remember." No, what I remember is that Blake and I had gotten used to going to Rock when things were shitty for us at home. Once Carla married him, she made it clear we were *not* welcome. She especially hated Heidi or basically any female who might be competition.

"Were you in the wedding?" she asks, dragging my head out of the past.

"Fuck no. She tried to discourage us from hanging around as much as possible."

"I'm sorry." She tilts her head, green eyes spearing me. Not in anger or pity. Disbelief maybe. "Well, you're always welcome at our house."

Yeah right.

"As soon as our kitchen's sorted, Heidi's supposed to come over to show me how to make applesauce. You'll have to come too."

The idea of my sister teaching Hope how to cook something so simple pushes some of my black mood away. Or maybe it's that she's still planning to do stuff with Heidi after the wedding. I guess I keep figuring at some point, Hope will drop the concerned mom bit she does with my sister. You know, when she doesn't need to impress Rock any more.

"There you are," Trinity yelps as she enters the kitchen. My heart thuds at the sight of her. Her messy blonde hair with different shades of blue at the ends, grazes her perfectly round ass. As ass I should absolutely *not* be staring at. She doesn't even notice I'm in the room at first.

They laugh and Trinity hipchecks Hope out of her way. "Teller needs coffee," Hope informs Trinity as she sits down across from me. "And we all know I suck at making coffee."

Trinity whips her head around, a quick smile lighting up her face. "Morning. Why are *you* up so early?"

"Need to go grab Heidi in a bit," I answer, focusing my attention on the window behind Hope.

"She could have joined our slumber party last night," Hope says.

Trinity snorts, and no matter how much I don't want to, I turn her way. "Nah, he doesn't want us corrupting his sister. You should hear the potty mouth on that girl," she says, pointing at Hope.

"Whatever." Hope snickers.

Tearing my gaze away from Trinity, I catch Hope's eye. "She said she had school work she wanted to get done last night so she didn't have to worry about it over the weekend. But it was probably an excuse for Axel to sneak over."

"I don't know," Hope says. "She's a pretty good student."

"I got your back, Teller," Trinity assures me. "I kept Axel out at the wedding site late last night hanging lights. Even if he did stop by, he would've been too exhausted to fool around."

Not the visual I needed. "Thanks, Trin."

"So, basically, everyone's seen the wedding site, but me?" Hope asks.

"Pretty much." Trinity turns and eyes Hope's toast. "You need to eat an egg or some other protein. I can't have you passing out at the altar."

"Okay, *Mom*. Geez."

"Morning, ladies."

I turn at the sound of my best friend's voice, relief washing over me. "Thank fuck, bro. I can't listen to any more of this girl shit or my nuts are going to shrivel up and fall off."

"What nuts?" Murphy asks with a straight face.

"Asshole."

Actually, I'd never admit it, but I was enjoying Trinity and Hope goofing around. Who am I kidding? I like being around Trinity no matter how I get her. "Where's your other friend, Hope? She sneak off to visit Z?"

Trinity shakes her head. "She was sound asleep when I woke up."

"Tell me there was at least one naked pillow fight last night?" Murphy laughs, so they know he's only kidding.

"You wish," Hope teases.

"That ain't right," he says, pulling out a chair and sitting next to me. He jabs his elbow against me.

"What?" He's tense, his gaze darting between the girls and me. "Spit it out."

"Nothing. We got church in twenty."

"Fuck."

Murphy raises an eyebrow. I never complain about club duties. But lately I'm feeling stretched thin.

"It'll be quick." Wrath's rumbling voice reaches us before he's even in the room. "There's my girl." He hooks an arm around Trinity's waist, and I turn away.

"Where's Heidi?" Murphy asks. *That's* enough to make me forget about the make-out session going on by the stove. Blake and I have been tighter than brothers for most of our lives, and I love him. Would do just about anything for Blake, but god*damn* am I getting tired of him sniffing after my baby sister like an unneutered dog.

"I gotta pick her up."

"When?"

"Right after church, apparently."

"Trinity," Hope calls out. "Should we bring Lilly breakfast?"

Trinity pulls away from Wrath a little dazed. "Sure." She probably didn't even hear the question.

"Uh-oh." Murphy laughs as Rock walks into the kitchen. Hope shrieks and jumps out of her chair when she sees him.

"No, no, no. You can't see me before the wedding."

Rock doesn't seem overly concerned with her outburst. His mouth slides into a smirk and he catches her around the waist. "You plannin' to wear this to the wedding?" he asks, pointing at her short, shiny robe and thin shorts.

"No."

"He can't see you in your *dress*, Hope," Trinity adds.

They're standing close enough to me that I hear Rock murmur to her, "Why are you running around like this?"

"Like what?"

Rock takes that as an invitation to molest her in front of everyone.

"Uh, prez. Some of us are trying to eat," Murphy jokes.

Hope backs away, nervously tugging at her robe, but Rock doesn't let her go far.

"For fuck's sake," Wrath groans. "Can't you save it for your wedding night?"

"You know, they say like sixty-five percent of couples end up not having sex on their wedding night," Trinity offers.

Everyone stares at her and she tips her head back, laughing. "I'm serious. They're too tired after all the wedding hoopla."

"No alcohol for you to tonight." Rock says it low, but we all hear it.

The kitchen lovefest is working my grouchiest nerve, so I make a few excuses and get the hell out of there. I'm moving so fast, I almost knock Mariella down outside the dining room.

"Sorry, hon."

Her big brown eyes stare up at me. "What's wrong?"

Something about Mariella always calms me down. The pressure in my chest eases, my shoulders drop. *Everything.* "A lot to do. Gonna be a busy day."

Her hands twist together in front of her. "I'm happy to be invited."

As if on cue, Hope's voice echoes behind me. "Good morning, Mariella."

"Happy wedding day," Mariella answers softly. She's always so damn nervous around Hope. I hate it, because no matter how many times I explain Hope doesn't hate her, Mariella doesn't believe me.

"Thank you."

"I better go help Trinity," Mariella says. Before she scurries away, I grab her hand.

"Come find me when you're done."

A brief smile flickers over her mouth. "I will." She slips from my grasp and darts away.

Next to me, Hope sighs. "Is she all right? You seem to be the only one she talks to."

"She's still worried you hate her—"

"I—"

"I know you don't."

Hope looks so troubled. Shit, if Rock finds out I upset

his bride on their wedding day, he'll fuckin' murder my ass. "Don't worry. I'll look out for her."

"Okay." Hope nudges my arm. "Tell Heidi to come see us when she gets here?"

"I will." Before she leaves, I want to do something to erase all my dickishness this morning. "Thank you." She raises an eyebrow. "For letting Heidi hang out with you and stuff."

"Teller, you don't have to keep thanking me. I really do enjoy spending time with her."

Christ, hanging out with the girls must have altered my brain chemistry or some shit. I clear my throat, thank her again, and take off before I do anything else to embarrass myself.

"ALL RIGHT," Rock shouts over the noise in the war room. "Simmer down. We don't have a lot of time."

We all find our seats or a place to stand. It's a full room because we have a lot of brothers from other charters here for the wedding.

Someone, probably Sway, slams his fist on the table and everyone follows, shouting congratulations at Rock.

The corners of his mouth turn up as he sits back in his seat and looks over each one of us. "Thank you. Thanks for being here." He nods at our guests. "I'm handing out assignments to my guys. And wanted to make our out-of-town brothers aware that we'll have members from two other clubs here as well. They're clubs we have solid business relationships with, so I don't expect any trouble."

That's Rock's diplomatic way of warning some of the punks in the group not to shoot at the sight of another club's colors on our property.

Murmurs of agreement go around the table.

Rock's phone buzzes and he slips it out of his cut. Flipping it open, he stares at it. His mouth twists in disgust and he flicks his gaze up. "Loco wants to meet."

"Now?" Wrath asks.

From the back, Sway laughs. "That fuck has the worst timing."

Z raises his hand. "I'll handle it, prez."

"Thanks."

"Now?"

"After we're done here." He points at Wrath and then Murphy. "Whisper and Merlin asked for a sit-down. I want you two to handle it."

Wrath's all seriousness this morning. "No problem, prez."

Next, Rock points to Z and Wrath. "Need you to talk to Stump and Chaser."

"Prez!" Sparky shouts even though he's only halfway down the table. "I got a package together for Stump. Something to ease him through this weird transition phase."

Rock's the only one who seems to be able to interpret that. "Thank you, brother. Work it out with them," he says, pointing to Wrath and Z again.

Even though Rock hasn't mentioned me yet, I know what my assignment's going to be. I asked him for it last night.

"Teller. I need you collecting any envelopes, keep the

prospects in line, and watch out for Mariella, please."

"No problem." I'm sure some of our brothers think Rock's punishing me by making me babysit a chick today. But since she's taking over Trinity's household stuff, Mariella's one of our most important assets. Since I'm still the only one she's comfortable around, it makes sense and I'm not insulted in the least.

"Hope's got civilian friends in the wedding. I expect everyone to behave." Rock says it like he's telling us, but *that* announcement's for our guests.

"She got any hot lawyer friends?" Shadow asks. He's a member of Sway's crew and hasn't met a pair of tits yet he didn't want to slip his dick between. His words, not mine. I'd describe him as a perverted fuckwad. Don't want him anywhere near my sister or Mariella.

"They're all married or involved," Z growls.

"So?" Shadow asks and cracks up at his own non-joke. *Idiot.*

Z catches my eye and shakes his head.

With a slap of his palm against the table, Rock ends church. "Let's do this."

On my way out, I stop by Rock's chair. "I need to pick Heidi up. I'll be back as soon as I can."

Rock stands and gives me a once over. "You look more stressed than I am. Simmer down, brother."

Wrath steps up behind Rock. "I'll be down here until you get back. Mariella will be fine," he says as if he knew exactly what was bothering me.

"Thank fuck, I thought you were going to hover over me all morning," Rock grumbles.

"Don't worry, I'll be up to babysit you later, prez."

Rock glares at him, and I can't help laughing.

Sway and Ghost, a president from one of our out-of-state charters, approach Rock. Wrath takes up a position behind our president, and I take the opportunity to hustle out of there.

"HEIDI! YOU READY?"

Giggling drifts out of her bedroom. I know Axel's at the property, so she's not in there with him. Heidi finally pokes her head out of her room, and in the background, I spot her friend Penny. Great. Just what I need.

"Hey."

"I sent you a text before I left the clubhouse. Why aren't you ready?"

"Oh." She ducks back into her room and comes out with her cell phone in her hand. "Sorry, I didn't see it."

"Are you kidding? You usually have it glued to your face."

She sticks her tongue out at me, and I crack a smile. "Come on. We need to go."

"Let me grab my dress and shoes."

In the two minutes Heidi's in her room, Penny approaches and runs her hand over my arm. "How do I get an invite to this wedding?" she asks in a low, I'm-sure-she-thinks-is-sexy, voice.

"You don't."

"Don't *you* need a date?"

"No," I growl in my best *fuck-off* voice. Christ, I've known Penny since she was a kid. I barely tolerate her hanging around my sister because I think she's a bad influence. I sure as fuck don't want to get involved with her—no matter how many times she tries.

"Ready!" Heidi announces, bursting into the living room. Her eyes narrow as she takes in how close Penny's standing to me and I take a step back.

Penny turns and rushes over to Heidi. They hug and screech as if they're not going to see each other for twenty years instead of a few hours.

"Heidi. Let's go."

"I'm coming. Calm yourself, bro." She smirks as she passes me, then stops and gives me a hug.

"You get your work done?" I ask, letting her go.

A more serious expression settles over her face. "I did. Now I have the whole weekend free."

Pride swells in my chest. Heidi drives me up the wall, but she's a good kid. Smart too.

The girls hug again outside and then I'm finally able to get Heidi on the road.

"Are you hanging with Mariella today?" she asks.

"Yeah, why?"

"She'll probably be freaked out with so many people up at the property."

My sister can be as sweet as she is smart. "She said she was looking forward to the wedding. But yeah, I'll stick with her."

"Who sticks with me?" she asks.

"I'll make sure Axel gets off prospect duty."

She bounces in her seat, clapping her hands. "Thank you."

Our drive goes by way too fast. Between her starting

college and spending all her free time with her boyfriend, and my club duties, I don't feel like I spend enough time with Heidi.

"Are you feeling wistful today?" she asks as I turn onto the road that leads to the clubhouse's driveway.

"Wistful? About what?"

"You know. Rock's getting married. Ever think about it yourself?"

I'm quiet for so long, she taps my arm. "Marcel?"

"I don't know." What's the point? Women leave or disappoint you eventually. But there's part of me that wonders what if... "Maybe."

"Yeah? You want to settle down?"

"One day."

"Have a few rugrats?"

"I already have a little rugrat."

She lets out an indignant snort. "You better not mean *me*."

I poke her side and she slaps my hand away. "Who else would I be talking about?"

"*Grr.* I'm trying to be serious." She's quiet for a few seconds. "You'd be a good dad. You've always taken good care of me," she says softly.

For a minute, I'm too choked up to respond. "Love you, Heidi." I glance over at her. "Why you worried about this stuff?"

"I want you to be happy."

"I'm happy." Before she says anything else, it occurs to me why I'm uneasy about this conversation. "The wedding isn't making you *wistful*, is it? You're too young to be worried about marriage."

She snorts. "No, big brother."

"Good. That's what I want to hear."

"I want to finish school. Find a good job, so I can afford to take lots and lots of vacations."

Her plans fill me with happiness. I want all of that for her. "Yeah? Where you plannin' on going?"

"Everywhere."

"That's my girl."

As soon as I stop the truck she flings the door open and jumps down. "Ugh, you need running boards on this beast," she grumbles.

"If you'd wait, I'd help you down."

She makes a wrinkled-nose growly face at me that's more cute than menacing.

I swat her toward the clubhouse. "Go get ready."

LEAVING Heidi in Murphy's care isn't ideal. He won't let anything happen to her. It's not that. No, it's the way he stared at her when she walked into the clubhouse that unnerved me. My sister had the biggest crush on him growing up and he hurt her more times than I can count by pushing her away. Now that she's almost eighteen, I don't want him getting any ideas. I love the club. I love my brothers. The more I think about it though, I don't want my sister caught up in the life. I saw how much Hope suffered this summer when Rock was in jail, and I don't ever want that for my sister.

Of course, if she's completely outside the club, that could leave her vulnerable to anyone looking to get at me.

It's a dilemma for another day. The current object of my sister's affection, one of our prospects, Axel, is busting his hump cleaning off all the stone benches where the wedding will take place. Ravage is busy supervising them and grins when he sees me.

"Prospect!" All three prospects snap their heads my way, and I fight back a grin. Pointing at Axel, I motion him closer.

He gives me the chance to speak first. "Finish helping out here. Once the wedding starts, you're off duty."

The corners of his mouth turn up slowly, like he's waiting for the punchline. "Actually, that's not true." I have to stop myself from laughing when his face falls. This kid needs a *lot* of work before he patches in to the club. "Your assignment is looking out for my sister."

"Oh. Yeah. Of course, I will. Is she here yet?"

"She's at the clubhouse doing her bridesmaid stuff."

His gaze darts to the woods, in the direction of the clubhouse.

"At ease, prospect. You'll see her soon enough."

"What's up, bro?" Ravage asks as he approaches. "You're hogging up my best worker."

"Hey," Hoot yells.

"Shut it, prospect," Ravage shouts back. When he faces me, he's laughing.

"After the wedding, his job is being my sister's date at the reception."

"Lucky fuck," Birch grumbles, just loud enough for me to hear.

My foot snaps out, catching him in the calf. "Watch your mouth."

"What? He gets to hang out with a hot chick all night while we're doing garbage duty?"

I glance at Ravage to see if he's as shocked as I am at Birch's disrespect. Ravage—the fucker—is laughing.

Getting up in Birch's space, I jab a finger in his chest. "My sister is not some *hot chick*. Stay the fuck away from her."

Ravage smacks the back of Axel's head. "Ain't you gonna stick up for your girl?"

Poor Axel looks confused as he glances at Ravage, me, and then Birch.

Birch glares at Ravage, and I realize what's going on. "Get back to work."

When they're busy, I throw a punch at Rav. "Think you're funny, dick?"

"What?" he asks with false innocence.

"What if I'd kicked his ass for that?"

"Oh, my money definitely would have been on you."

"Asshole."

"Lighten up."

"Where's Dex?"

"'Round here somewhere."

As if he has some sixth sense, Dex strolls into the amphitheater. "'Sup, brother?"

"Can you sit with Mariella during the wedding?"

"Yeah. No problem. Swan's up at the house with her now."

I slap Ravage's chest a little harder than necessary and bump fists with Dex before leaving.

Mariella's not in the living room, but I know where to find her. The kitchen.

The clubhouse dining room's packed with visiting brothers being rowdy as fuck, and the women who joined them. I stop to say hello to brothers I haven't seen in a while, but I'm not in the mood to shoot the shit right now, so I keep moving toward the kitchen.

Swan and Mariella are working side-by-side, cracking eggs, whipping them up and tossing food onto plates. The two of them seem to have a system down.

"Everything good down at the site?" Wrath asks from the table by the window.

"Yeah. Why ain't you out there?" I ask, jerking my thumb over my shoulder toward the dining room.

He waves his hand in the air. "Told you I'd look out for her," he says, nodding at Mariella. "Besides, not in the mood for socializing."

"Are you ever?"

"No."

Tawny, Sway's ol' lady, slams open the kitchen door and enters the room in her typical *I-own-everything-in-my-path* style. A few other ol' ladies follow behind her. "Where can we help?" she asks.

Mariella seems absolutely terrified of Tawny. Swan glances up and then back to what she was working on. Swan's rarely ruffled by anyone.

Wrath stands and points to the trays the girls set aside. "I think that stuff was going out next," he says.

"We're on it." Tawny directs the girls. "How's Rock? Nervous?" she asks Wrath.

He lifts his shoulders. "Gonna go check on him now." He leaves without making it too obvious he wants to get away from Tawny.

I hold out my hand. "Mariella, I need your help." She throws a look of relief at me. Tawny doesn't know what Mariella's role is here. I'm sure she thinks she's another clubwhore for Tawny to boss around, and I want her to understand I won't tolerate that bullshit.

"My girls and I can take over if you want, Teller."

"Sure. Swan, Dex is looking for you."

"Oh." She wipes her hands down the front of her apron, then tosses it in the laundry bin.

"I got it, sweetheart," Tawny says, shooing us out of the kitchen.

Swan skirts the crowd in the dining room and disappears into the hallway. Mariella and I take the slow route, while I make sure every brother here knows she's with me.

Okay, not *with me* in the sense they're thinking. But no one needs to know that.

"How you doing, sweetheart?" I ask once we're in the hallway. She peers up at me and a small smile tugs the corners of her mouth up. "Good."

Together, we walk up the stairs and I drop her off at her room. "I'll be back in fifteen."

"I'll be ready."

I jog down to my room, clean up and change, then head back to Mariella.

She opens the door before I knock and I freeze. Normally, she hides behind her long curtain of dark hair and baggy sweats. For the wedding, she's twisted her hair up into a sexy-messy pile. She's wearing some sort of loose, flowy dress in earthy colors with short bell sleeves.

The dress stops a few inches above her knees, showing off her bare legs.

"You look beautiful."

She tilts her head down and runs her hands over the dress. "Thank you. Trinity helped me pick it out."

"It's nice."

She takes my hand, and I lead her downstairs. "Dex and Swan are gonna hang with you while I'm doing my wedding stuff, okay?"

"Teller. I'm sorry. You don't have to keep watch over me. I'm sure you'd rather…socialize…"

"Hey." I stop and tug her hand, spinning her to face me. "The only 'socializing' I want to do is with you."

"You must want to spend time with other girls—"

"Stop. Not today."

"All right. I don't want you to be mad at me later, though."

I reach out and rub my thumb over her cheek. "Stop worrying about stuff that's never gonna happen."

NOT THAT I give a lot of thought to these things, but the wedding's damn near perfect. I'm happy Rock's found someone to care about. Hopefully, they last.

My sister's beautiful. So damn grown up I can barely look at her. After the wedding, I keep her close. It annoys her at first, but she's used to my hovering.

As the sun sets, and the crowd gets rowdier, I lean over to Heidi. "I want you to head back to the clubhouse."

"Let me say good night to Rock and Hope? Please?"

"Yeah. Of course." When she's gone, I pin Axel with my *I'll-murder-you-if-anything-happens-to-my-sister* face. "Watch her."

"Always," he answers.

Across the room, I spot Murphy and give him a nod.

"Ready to go?" I ask Mariella.

She all but jumps out of her chair. "Yes."

On the way back to the clubhouse, she doesn't have a lot to say, but she stops me in the front yard. "It's such a pretty night, can we stay out here a little longer?"

"Sure." I nod at one of the stone benches and she perches on the edge, then tips her head back to stare at the sky.

"You want to go for a ride?"

"No."

One of these days, I'll get her to say yes.

People drift in and out of the clubhouse. Some stop and talk to us.

"Hi, Marcel," my sister shouts. Next to me, Mariella laughs softly.

Heidi excitedly explains that Axel's taking her for a moonlit ride. I'm less than thrilled, but Axel promises to be careful.

After they leave, Mariella sighs. "She's so sweet. You're lucky to have each other."

"I didn't always think so." I wish I'd chosen better words. As I finish the sentence, I remember Mariella's brother was a dirtbag who sold her off to the Vipers MC to pay off a debt. Reaching over, I take her hand and squeeze.

"Don't feel bad for me, Teller."

"I don't." I glance over at her. "I'm happy you're here."

"So am I." She lets out a soft yawn.

"You want to head upstairs?"

"I think so. I was up early."

I'm not ready to say good night to her when we reach her door, but I do. Leaning over, I lay a swift kiss on her cheek, then back away.

Outside, I stroll the grounds by myself for a while. When I return, Axel's bike's still in the parking lot.

"Tha fuck?"

"YOU SEEN HEIDI?" I ask Murphy. If anyone seems to always know where she is, it's him.

"A little while ago. Why?"

"She was supposed to be going for a ride with Axel. But his bike's still here."

A flash of anger, hurt, jealousy, something like that crosses his face and he jerks his chin toward the door of the room she uses when she stays here. Storming over, I bang on it a few times. When I look for Murphy he's all the way down the hall going into his room. "Big help," I grumble.

There's rustling, a low murmur, and noises on the other side of the door, so I bang on it again.

Heidi throws it open, nervously running her hands through her hair. "Oh. Hey, big brother, what's up?"

Yeah, Heidi never greets me like that. Obviously, they were up to something. Looking past her, I find Axel sitting on the bed, staring at his feet.

"I thought you two were going for a ride?"

"We are. We were just hanging out."

I'm torn. No doubt, in a couple hours, the party will move to the clubhouse. I don't want Heidi around here for whatever dirty shit my brothers get into. But I also don't want her taking off and spending the night with this little punk.

"It's gettin' late." Axel hasn't been riding long enough that I feel comfortable with him taking my sister out on the back roads around here. I think the little shit realizes that's what I'm implying.

"I'm always careful with her," he says.

Heidi's jaw clenches, but she doesn't argue with me, thank fuck.

"All right, all right, we're going." As she turns around, I swear she mumbles something that sounds like, "Rather do it in my bed anyway," but I ignore it.

I ever actually *catch* them in the act, it will be a different story. One where Axel ends up with bullet in his crotch.

Axel stands, and she grabs her leather jacket. "Are you going to stand in my doorway the whole time?"

Christ, she makes me crazy. Even if she's almost an adult, she'll always be my baby sister.

I follow the two of them downstairs, but instead of being annoyed by my overbearing ass, Heidi turns before getting on Axel's bike and wraps her arms around me. "Are you going to get some rest? You look tired," she says softly. Her eyes search my face and she doesn't seem to like what she sees.

"I'm fine. I won't rest until you call and tell me you're home safe, though."

"Are you coming home?"

"I gotta stay up here and make sure things don't get out of control." I look past her and point at Axel. "That's not an invitation for *you* to stay over."

He holds his hands out in an innocent *who me?* way that doesn't fool me one bit.

"I'll send someone by to check on you."

She rolls her eyes. "Don't you dare. I'm fine."

Shouting from the woods keeps getting closer. Party's moving toward the clubhouse. I want to get inside and check on Mariella. Maybe I should insist Heidi spend the night here instead. If I thought she'd stay in her room and out of trouble, I would.

"Would you rather stay up here?" I ask her.

Her mouth twists and she cocks her head to the side. Toward the noise in the woods. "Normally, I'd say yes, but…"

"Yeah, that's what I thought."

She grabs me again for another hug, and I hang on to her longer than I'm sure she'd like me to in front of her boyfriend, but I don't give a fuck.

Axel shakes my hand, and they take off.

I'm not sure why I have such an ache in my chest watching her go.

AS I PUSH through the crowd in the living room to get to the stairway, Sparky waves me over. Not surprisingly, he's high as fuck. "Heidi okay?" he asks. He's always had a soft spot for Heidi. Not in a creepy way. More like the protective way he worries over his plants.

"Yeah, Axel just took her home."

"Oh, good. She's good for him."

"Yeah? He good for her?"

"Don't know yet, man."

I hold my hand out and he misses bumping my fist by about a foot. Shaking my head, I sprint up the stairs. At the top, I hesitate. I want to check on Mariella, but I don't want to bother her if she's sleeping.

A muffled cry comes from her room.

Jesus Christ, if something happened to her when I was supposed to be watching—

I knock on her door. A few light taps at first. With all the noise going on, the cry could have come from somewhere else.

There's another one, and this time it's definitely from her room. I knock harder.

Her door swings open. Light from the hallway spills over her face, red and tear-stained.

"What's wrong? Did someone bother you?"

"No," she answers softly.

"I didn't mean to wake you. I thought I heard something."

Her cheeks turn even redder. "I still have...I still can't."

Reaching out, I place my hand on her shoulder, pulling her closer. "What?"

"Nightmares. Every night. Even though today was such a good day. They never stop."

Shit.

"I'm sorry."

She shakes her head and tries to back away. I hate knowing she's suffering like this. "Is there anything I can do?"

"You've already done so much for me. Thank you." I tighten my hold on her shoulder and turn to check the hallway.

"Do you want to come stay in my room? Not for…just for…you know, tonight?" Christ, I've never had so much trouble getting a woman in my room before. Getting them *out*, sure.

"No. You don't want me. What if you…?"

I snort because she's the only girl who's interested me since she moved in. I know how traumatized she still is from her time with the Vipers MC, so I won't *do* anything about it. Doesn't mean I don't want to.

Right now, though, I just want to do something to give her some peace. "Come on. You know you're safe with me," I say, piling on what Blake always calls my "Teller charm" by lowering my voice and pulling her a little closer.

"If you're sure? I do think I'd feel better."

She ducks back in her room and grabs her pillows and a blanket, then lets me lead her down the hallway.

My room's neat and clean, the way I left it. Mariella crawls into bed immediately, tucking herself in the corner with her back to the wall. "Good?" I ask.

"Yes, thank you."

A few minutes later I slip under the covers. It kills me, but I keep my distance. I'm hovering around the edge of sleep, when something soft bumps against me. Startled, I open my eyes. I can't make anything out in the dark, but I feel Mariella next to me. "You okay?" I whisper.

She doesn't answer.

Christ, she smells good. Like cinnamon and coconuts. I want to bury my face against her neck and kiss—

This is a problem.

Afraid she'll wake up with my morning wood tucked against her ass, I stuff an extra pillow in the space between us. I wrap an arm around her waist, pulling her close.

Somehow I will myself to go to sleep.

Mariella

For the first time in a very long time, I feel safe.

In my sleep, I must have twisted and found my way next to Teller. As if my body trusts him to keep me from harm.

"You okay?" he whispers.

I don't know how to answer him, so I pretend to be asleep. His warmth soaks into my back, relaxing and comforting.

He shifts and something soft presses into my back.

A pillow.

A barrier between us.

Did he do that so I'd feel protected?

Or does he think I'm used and disgusting and wants some distance between us?

I have my answer a few seconds later.

He gently pushes the hair off my cheek and kisses my temple, murmuring, "You're safe with me, Mariella."

MURPHY

TODAY'S a big day for the Upstate charter of the Lost
Kings MC.

Our Prez found his Queen and he's locking her down
tight. It's the first wedding we've held at our clubhouse
and everyone's working to make sure things are perfect
for prez and his first lady. I was up early discussing our
agenda for church with Rock and then rounding up the
brothers for the meeting.

Now I'm waiting for my best friend to get his ass to
the clubhouse. I really want to see Heidi before we get
swept up in all the wedding stuff.

I catch a glimpse of Teller's truck through the front
window.

Finally.

Heidi walks in first. A dress covered in plastic draped
over her arm. Like an idiot I stare at her for a minute
without saying anything. I swear she's more beautiful
every time I see her. "Ready for your trip down the aisle,
Bug?"

The corners of her mouth lift as she approaches and
lets me wrap her up in a hug. Behind her, Teller rolls his
eyes and points a finger-gun at his head. I'm guessing
Heidi gave him grief this morning. As her eighteenth
birthday's barreling down on him, he's finally realized
trying to control her is a battle he won't win.

"You're walking with me?" she asks.

I'm so caught up in the feel of her against me. Her scent surrounding me that it takes me a second to process the question and answer it. "Hell, yeah. You didn't want to walk with your brother, did you?"

Soft laughter flows out of her and she covers her mouth with her hand the way she's done since she was a kid. "No."

Teller's watching us with narrowed eyes, and I reluctantly pull away from Heidi. He gives me a chin lift. "I promised Trinity I'd go check on the prospects out at the site."

"Okay."

He tilts his head toward Heidi in a *watch her* gesture Heidi absolutely notices. "I'm not a kid. I don't need a babysitter."

"I ain't a babysitter," I tease. Teller glares at me again. *Can I trust you with my baby sister or not?* his face seems to say. We've been best friends so long, I can pretty much figure out what he's thinking. I nod at him and he heads out to the site where the wedding's taking place.

Members from our downstate charter and a couple other LOKI charters are here for the wedding. Two clubs we're friendly with are also attending, so whether Teller asked or not, today is a day I absolutely plan to look out for Heidi. When we were kids, Teller protected me when no one else would. In turn, I've always had his back. Together, we've always looked out for Heidi. That will never change, no matter how old we are.

By age eight, I'd already lived a life full of disappointment and turmoil. She doesn't remember, because she was only a baby, but Heidi was the sweetest thing in my world. She made it impossible not to love her. Teller and I did our best to provide her with everything her parents should have and failed.

Even today, I'd kill anyone who hurt her.

I love her. I can't *have* her because she's only seventeen and I'm twenty-five. She's made it damn hard too.

Or at least she used to. Before her boyfriend Axel wormed his way into her life.

"Are you okay?" she asks, glancing up at me with the sweetest, concerned expression on her face.

While she can be a hellraiser when she wants to be, Heidi also has the biggest heart of anyone I know.

She twists her hands into the plastic covering her dress nervously, and I realize I'm still staring at her like an idiot.

"Yeah."

"Oh." A nervous smile flickers over her lips.

"That the dress?" Unfortunately, I'd had to escort the girls to the dress shop. I bitched about it mightily, but I got to spend time with Heidi, so it wasn't all bad.

She glances down at the bag. "Yes. I'll probably look silly."

I doubt that. I may know fuck-all about dresses, but she could wear a pair of coveralls and still be the most beautiful girl in any room.

"You're beautiful no matter what," I finally answer.

"Thank you."

"Are you excited?"

"Oh, yes. I love Hope so much. I'm so happy she'll be an official part of the family now. She and Uncle Rock are so perfect together."

Her enthusiasm makes me smile. Hope's sort of mothered Heidi since the day they met. Something Heidi's never had, but always needed.

"Have you seen Axel today?"

My jaw tightens at the sound of his name. "Yeah, he's down at the site doing last minute decorations, cleaning and stuff."

"Oh. Where's Hope?"

"Down in Trinity's room, I think."

She raises the arm her dress is draped over. "I should probably go put this on."

"Yeah, okay."

"I'll see you later."

Heidi

"KNOCK, KNOCK."

I've never been in Trinity's room and I'm not sure I'm welcomed now.

The door swings open, and Hope's friend Lilly waves me inside. "Yay! Heidi's here," Lilly yells.

I'm still rattled from the way Murphy's gaze roamed over me out in the living room. No, rattled isn't quite the right word. Warm and tingly?

"Hi, Heidi," Hope greets.

"Don't move," Trinity warns. "Hey, Heidi," she says without looking at me. She's focused on lining Hope's eyes with dark brown eyeliner. A bunch of nail polish is lined up on the desk next to them. One's a glittering gold that I'm instantly jealous of. I glance down at my own short nails. Last night, I'd painted them a bright plum to match my dress, but now I wish I'd thought of something more fun.

"Are you sure the polish will dry? Shouldn't we do that first?" Hope asks as Trinity starts sponging foundation over Hope's forehead.

It must not be the first time she's asked. "Yes," Trinity answers with exaggerated patience.

Hope tilts her head at the space next to her. "Come. Sit. Tell me what you're up to."

"She's nervous," Lilly whispers to me.

Trinity sets the foundation down and picks up one small clear bottle. "Shit. My fast-dry topcoat is hard as a rock." Trinity bites her lip as she keeps trying to wiggle the brush around.

"What's the closest store? I'll go grab another bottle," Lilly offers.

"Are you sure?"

Lilly rolls her eyes. "Yes."

Trinity writes down the directions to Wards. The clubhouse is so far out in the country, it will take Lilly at least an hour to drive there and back.

"Don't move. I'll be back. Heidi do you want to come with me?"

"No, thank you."

"You can use my bathroom to change if you want," Trinity says.

After closing myself inside, I pull the dress out and inspect it for wrinkles or lint. It's one-shouldered, so I had to buy a special bra for it, but it's the most grown-up thing in my closet.

Once I'm finally in it, I need someone to help with the zipper. "Trinity?" I call out.

She opens the door and I don't even have to ask, she automatically moves behind me and pulls up the zipper.

"Perfect," she says.

"Are you sure?"

"Yes."

"Oh, Heidi! It looks so pretty," Hope gushes when I come out.

"Thanks."

They go back to last minute wedding talk, and there are a few dirty jokes that I'm pretty sure are in reference to my uncles Rock and Wrath—*ew*.

"I'm starving. Do you mind if I go grab something to eat?"

"Not at all. You know where to find us," Hope says with a giggle. I guess she's nervous.

"Do you want me to bring something back for you guys?"

Both of them say no.

This end of the clubhouse is surprisingly quiet, considering the big event that's about to happen. I'd kind of like to say hi to Uncle Rock, but I'm not sure if he's upstairs or out at the wedding site.

As I'm about to step into the dining room, I run into Murphy.

"Sorry." He reaches out to steady me with a hand on my waist. "Wow." The way he stares at me heats my skin and I pull out of his grasp.

Murphy

FOR SEVERAL LONG, uncomfortable seconds, I forget how to breathe. I stare at Heidi for so long, she fidgets, nervously tugging at the skirt of her dress.

"Stop," I say, reaching out to still her hand.

"It looks awful, doesn't it?"

Absolutely not. I may know fuck-all about dresses, but it's perfect on her. "No. You're gorgeous, Heidi. That's a pretty color on you."

Her cheeks flush and she glances down at her feet. "Thanks."

I'm not lying. The purple suits her dark hair and eyes. The bare shoulders and skirt that falls right above her knees aren't too bad either. But it's the damn top of the dress, fitted tight to her curves, that's making me edgy.

Curves I shouldn't be noticing.

Curves I don't want anyone else noticing.

I'm so quiet, she twists her hands in her skirt again.

Words. Where are my fucking words? *Fuck.* I saw her in the dress when she bought it, but somehow she looks so…different now. "You're beautiful. I'm just not used to you looking so grown-up, that's all."

"Oh." Her face brightens, and I feel like an ass for making her doubt herself for even a second.

I finally manage to shake myself out of my stupor. "Why aren't you with the bride?"

"I'm hungry. I had breakfast, but it was hours ago."

"Let's get you some food then."

Slinging one arm around her shoulders, I pull her to

my side and walk her through the dining room and into the kitchen.

"I have something for you."

Her eyes widen. "You do?"

"Yup." Opening the fridge, I dig around until I find the container I hid in the back so no one would touch it.

God help me, but she bounces up and down on her toes. It physically hurts to tear my gaze away.

"What is it? What is it?" she yelps. My Heidi has always loved presents of any kind.

I set the container on the counter and pop the lid off, revealing a batch of plump chocolate covered strawberries.

"Oh my God!" she squeals. "They're so pretty!"

"Trinity made them for their sleepover last night. I asked her to set some aside for you."

Her pretty brown eyes blink a few times. "Thank you." She hesitates. "Maybe I should eat some real food first."

"Good call." I end up making us sandwiches while she watches and critiques my sandwich-making skills. We take our plates to the small table by the window. That way I can keep an eye out for anyone who's going to intrude on our time.

She only ends up eating half of her sandwich, pushing her plate toward me. "Berry time!"

I nudge the container to her side and finish her sandwich.

"Hmm…they all look good. I don't know where to start."

I chuckle while she makes her decision as if it's life or death.

I'm not laughing a few second later when strawberry juice lands in her cleavage.

No, I'm biting my tongue so I don't lick the drop from her skin.

"Oh. Crap." She wipes it away, sucking her finger and seriously testing my control.

"Better be careful. Don't wanna ruin your dress." I grind the words out and hand her a paper towel.

"Yeah, I'm not used to so much skin showing." She waves her hand over her boobs, as if I need the reminder. "Good thing, though or I totally would have stained my dress."

I've never felt the meaning of "no good deed goes unpunished" as acutely as I do in the next fifteen minutes while I watch her carefully work through half the berries.

"Don't you want any?" she asks.

"Sure."

She ends up handing me one and having me eat it out of her hand. Isn't that appropriate?

"I can't believe Trin made these. They must take forever. They're soooo good though."

"She seemed to have a system down. Mariella helped her."

She nods and stands, carrying the rest of the berries back to the refrigerator. I wait and watch her at the sink, washing her hands. Hell, I'll pretty much sit and watch Heidi do anything.

When she's finished, she turns and flashes a sweet smile. "Thank you."

"You know I'm always thinking of you."

Her smile fades. "I know."

Time to lighten things back up. "Can I steal you away from the bridal party a little longer?" I ask, holding out my hand.

"Sure."

I have one final thing to give her, waiting in the living room behind the bar.

"Is Axel still helping to get things ready?" she asks, waving her hand toward the woods.

My stomach twists at the sound of her boyfriend's name. "Yeah." Axel wouldn't be getting off prospect duty any time soon if I had any say.

What I'd stupidly forgotten was, a couple weeks ago, I'd invited Serena to the wedding. A fact that's bound to bite me in the ass soon. As I'm about to grab Heidi's present, I glance out the window and spot Serena walking toward the front door. She notices me and waves.

Fuck.

"Hi, Murphy," Serena calls out as she walks inside.

"Hey." I motion for her to stay where she is. But it's too late. Heidi turns and figures it out immediately. Her face crumples with disappointment.

"I should go see if Hope needs anything," she says softly.

Serena approaches me slow. A dress slung over her arm. "Do you mind if I change in your room?"

My gaze returns to Heidi, who hasn't looked up or moved or anything. Her reddened cheeks signal she's either about cry or blow up.

"Yeah, sure," I finally answer Serena's question.

"Later," Heidi says, moving past me without another word.

"Is everything okay?" Serena asks.

I rip my attention away from Heidi, hurrying away from us.

"Yeah. Same old shit."

Heidi

YOU HAVE A BOYFRIEND. It doesn't matter.

I keep repeating those two sentences to myself as I sprint down the hallway to Trinity's room.

It's not like I haven't seen Murphy with girls over the years. Each one had been a tiny knife jammed in my heart. But this one spoke to him in such a familiar way. Like they spend a lot of time together.

So why was he busy saving strawberries for me? Being so sweet to me? If he had a girl coming?

Not a girl. A *woman*. Probably closer to his age. I barely looked at her. Only long enough to note she was tall and pretty, with her blonde hair all elegantly pulled up into some complicated updo. *Poised* my grandmother would have called her. Not a messy teenager stuffed into a dress that's too fancy for her.

I hesitate before knocking on Trinity's door again.

Someone shouts for me to come in and I poke my head inside the room. Hope's finally in her dress instead of the bathrobe she was in earlier. "Am I allowed to hang out in here?"

"Of course, sweetheart." Hope waves her hands in welcome, and I close the door behind me.

Lilly's back and Hope's friend, Mara is also here. I

murmur hellos to both of them and put my back against the wall, so I'm out of the way.

"Everything okay?" Mara asks.

"Yeah." I finally glance up and smile. I don't want to do anything to ruin Hope's day. "You look so pretty, Hope."

"Thank you." She grabs a bag and starts tearing through it. "Hold on."

Trinity swipes two boxes off her desk and taps Hope's shoulder.

Hope hands one box to me and one to Mara. "Thank-you presents for being such wonderful bridesmaids."

I feel a little guilty taking anything, since technically I don't think I've done much to help Hope with the wedding.

Inside, I find a pair of long, amethyst earrings. They dangle and sparkle. "They're so pretty. I don't have dangly ones like this. Grams never let me wear them."

Hope flashes a relieved smile. "Good."

I stand in front of the mirror to put them in, but my hair hides them, unless I brush it off my shoulders. "I wish I was wearing my hair up now."

Trinity moves behind me, picking up my hair in one hand. "I can help you put it up if you want," she offers.

"I'd love it. Thanks," I finally answer.

While Trinity tugs, yanks, and—*ouch*—pins my hair into submission, I watch Hope laughing with her friends.

"What's wrong, honey?" she asks, meeting my eyes in the mirror.

"Nothing. Did you know Murphy was bringing a date?"

Her mouth twists down and her gaze slips to the side. "He mentioned it when I was doing the invitations."

"Oh. Do you know her?"

"I've met her. She's a nice girl."

Nice girl. She's met her before? This girl's in Murphy's life enough that he took the time to introduce her to Hope?

"Is your boyfriend in the wedding?" Mara asks me.

Boyfriend. Yup. Remember him? "Yes. Sort of," I answer just as Trinity slides the one last bobby pin home.

"All done. What do you think?"

"It's so pretty! Thank you, Trinity."

Trinity spends an eternity taking photos of all of us while Hope and her friends goof around. It's funny seeing this side of them.

Uncle Z knocks on the door when it's time for the wedding to start.

I follow everyone out front, hanging back because I don't want to see Murphy again. I can't stand the thought of holding his arm while we walk down the aisle.

For Hope I'll do it. If it was anyone else, I think I would have locked myself in the bathroom by now.

Trinity hands us mini bouquets of jewel-toned flowers wrapped in ribbon and accented with crystals on the handles. "These are so pretty."

"Thanks, I finished them up early this morning."

"Is there anything you can't do, Trinity?" Lilly asks.

Embarrassed, Trinity shrugs.

My brother strides over and pulls me away from the girls for a hug. "Look at you. You're so pretty, baby sis."

"Thank you." I squeeze him back hard. My emotions

are flipping out so I end up clinging to him longer than the situation requires. While we're hugging, one of the UTVs starts up. Z has the bigger vehicle, so he takes Hope, Lilly, and Trinity out to the site. Teller steps back and says hello to Mara. "Your husband's out there with the groom, so I'm your ride." He flashes a bright smile and Mara laughs.

"Lucky me." It really sounds more like she's humoring my brother than flirting with him. Thank God. Because watching women fawn over my brother is just...*ew*.

"You okay, Heidi?" my brother asks after escorting Mara to his vehicle.

"I'll be fine."

He glances at Murphy and the two share some unspoken message, because Murphy nods.

After my brother takes off, Murphy swaggers over. "We don't have a lot of time. I wanted to give you this, though."

He holds out a box with a flower and some feathers in it. "A wrist corsage?"

He shrugs, almost looking embarrassed. "I thought you'd like it."

The peacock feathers are dyed purple to match my dress and accent a blue and purple orchid. He obviously put a lot of thought into it. "It's beautiful." My voice comes out barely above a whisper.

He takes it out of the box and slips it over my hand. "Perfect."

My fingers stroke the silky feathers. "You remembered the color of my dress?"

"How could I forget?"

I finally raise my gaze to meet his eyes. "Thank you."

He doesn't say anything, just nods and escorts me to our UTV.

"Is your girlfriend already out there?"

His jaw tightens, but he doesn't answer my question.

Guess it's going to be a bumpy ride.

Murphy

HEIDI'S KNOCKED me on my ass twice today. When I first saw her in that dress and again when she came out with the girls.

When she asks about Serena, I want to crawl in a hole. If she were any other girl, I'd give her a slick answer and a smirk. But this is Heidi. She's more than the girl I'm in love with but can't have. She's also my friend.

"Don't worry about it," I finally answer.

She snorts and turns her head, watching the woods. I wish we had more time together, but we arrive at the wedding spot quick. Everyone else is assembled and waiting for us.

"What took so long, dick?" Wrath growls at me. "Go get in line before Trinity rips your head off."

Rock walks Hope up front, and we take our places next to them.

"Welcome, everyone," Damon begins. "I'm honored to be here to celebrate the beginning of what we know will be an extraordinary marriage. Rochlan and Hope, to choose marriage is to accept a challenge." Rock grins at Hope and she playfully swats him. "Things won't always be easy, but you both share a commitment to putting each other first in both difficult times and wonderful times, growing stronger with each shared experience. Marriage is a journey, not a destination and although neither of you will always be perfect, you are perfect for one another."

There's so much in there that hits me in the chest. For Rock, who I love like a surrogate father. For Hope, who I've grown to care for and would die to protect. The reminder that life itself is a journey and finding the right person to spend it with makes all the difference.

Across the way, Heidi's watching me, and the corners of my mouth turn up. She returns the smile, then glances away.

I spend the rest of the ceremony staring at her and wondering if one day this will be us.

Heidi

I HAVE A BELLY full of honey bees as I watch Rock marry Hope. My head's spinning with so many thoughts.

"…you both share a commitment to putting each other first in both difficult times and wonderful times, growing stronger with each shared experience." Damon's words hit me in the deepest parts of my soul.

Every now and then, I flick my gaze a few feet to the right and catch Murphy watching me. There was a time in my life where I used to dream of marrying him in a ceremony very much like this one.

Childish daydreaming.

Another few feet to the right and my gaze lands on my

boyfriend, Axel. His mouth curves into a quick smile. Behind him, in the crowd, I spot Murphy's date. Jealousy squeezes my heart, and my gaze moves back to Axel.

Before I know it, we're setting boxes of pretty orange and black butterflies free, and then the ceremony's over. Hope promised it would be quick, and it was. I'm pulled into a bunch of group photos. Many of them where I have to stand next to Murphy.

When we're finally set free, Axel meets me at the edge of the group. "You were the prettiest one up there," he says before leaning down to kiss my cheek.

"Thank you," I murmur.

His gaze strays to my wrist corsage. "Where'd that come from?"

Even though I know I'm risking pissing Axel off, I won't lie to him. "Murphy gave it to me."

"What'd you do, complain to him that I never got you one for prom?"

"Jeez, no."

Because he knows that was a dick thing to say, he cracks a quick smile and plays it off like he was only kidding. It's too beautiful a day, too happy an occasion, to waste it arguing, so I let it go. Axel takes my hand and leads me into the tent. Trinity didn't bother with seating arrangements. The only table that's off-limits is the one set up in front for the bride and groom.

"Heidi!" Someone calls out, and I turn to find Tawny coming at me. Arms open wide for a hug. "How are you, baby? I haven't seen you since—" She stops abruptly, her smile fading as she remembers she hasn't seen me since my grandmother's funeral.

"I'm okay. How are you?" I'm pulled in for a hug, pressed tight to her squishy chest and forced to inhale her smoky-perfume scent for what feels like a *really* long time. Finally, I shake free and force a big smile. "Wasn't the wedding beautiful?"

"Yes. It's so good she's an official part of the family now. She's good for Rock," Tawny says. I sort of doubt Uncle Rock was overly worried about Tawny's seal of approval.

Tawny's gaze rakes over my boyfriend, and next to me, I feel him quiver. I take his hand, pulling him a little closer. "I was planning to sneak my boyfriend away before someone puts him to work," I say which makes Tawny laugh.

"You're still with the club, Axel. That's good," she says. She spends a few too many seconds eye-fondling him before turning to talk to someone else. I'm not jealous. More grossed-out. She's old enough to be his mom. In fact, I'm pretty sure both her children are older than Axel.

Axel leans over and whispers in my ear. "She freaks me the fuck out."

I burst out laughing, and we continue over to the drink station. My brother's camped out there, making it impossible for me to sneak any alcohol—not that I would anyway, but jeez. He gives both of us a stern look and points to the table closest to him. "We're sitting there, little sister."

He ignores my eye-roll and keeps staring me down, letting me know it's not up for discussion. Axel shrugs, I don't think he cares where we sit as long as he's not fetching things for anyone. Marcel and Mariella join us, so at least I don't feel like my brother tried to sit us at the kiddy table or something. Mara and Damon sit with us too. Strangely, the conversation flows easily. My brother seems to know Damon well, and respect him—and it's not easy to earn my brother's respect, so that's interesting.

Leaning over, I catch Damon's eye. "I really liked what you said at the wedding. About marriage being a journey and being imperfectly perfect for each other."

He tilts his head to the side, as if he's surprised I was paying attention during the ceremony.

But, I captured each and every word, locking them in my memory.

"I try to tailor my opening words to each couple, and that theme seemed appropriate," he says.

"It was."

Everyone talks about the ceremony, the butterflies, what a perfect autumn day it is for a wedding.

The food is arranged so we can grab whatever we want from the buffet whenever we want, which makes the party feel relaxed and easy. People mingle and chat. If I had to guess, I'd say a number of business deals were going on between the different LOKI charters attending the wedding. I also recognize patches from other MCs that I know have had a long history with the club.

That's not stuff *I'm* supposed to notice, so I concentrate on my plate and absorb the happiness of being surrounded by family.

Murphy

THE WEDDING'S a happy occasion for our prez. For the rest of us, there's business to conduct. We're leaving Rock out of it, but no doubt he'll press us for details tomorrow.

Wrath and I are up first to meet with the Wolf Knights. They seriously fucked us over by being sloppy. Rock spent the summer in jail because of their fuck-up. Our meeting will cover how they plan to compensate us.

In our world, the payment will be in either blood or money.

If we feel what their offering is in any way disrespectful, then it will be a bloody conversation.

"Ready?" Wrath asks.

Serena's busy talking to some girls she knows from Sway's charter. Rock's wrapped up in his new bride. Heidi's, well she's with her boyfriend, so I'm trying not to pay attention to Heidi.

I need to focus.

"Let's do this." I pat the Glock 27 at my hip and follow Wrath. We meet Whisper, the SAA for the Wolf Knights, and Wrath's business partner right outside the tent.

"Merlin's coming too," Whisper says after shaking both our hands.

We don't bother with small talk. Merlin shows up, and Wrath leads us back down to where we held the wedding. There's lots of stone benches and a wide stone altar to use as a table if we need it.

It's also out of the way in case we need to hide a body for a couple hours.

Wrath leads us down to the table and takes up a position behind it. I stand to his right. Whisper's across

from me and Merlin's across from Wrath. Tonight, I'm
basically acting as SAA, here to watch Wrath's back.

My brother plays it the way he always does. Quiet. He
stands and crosses his arms over his chest, staring Merlin
down, but not saying anything. It's a tactic I've seen him
use many times.

It always works.

"Are we cool?" Merlin asks after a few uncomfortable
seconds pass.

Wrath's expression doesn't change. "You tell me."

Merlin slips his hand inside his cut and my hand
twitches toward my right hip. The movement's subtle.
Neither of them notice. Wrath catches my eye and gives
me the briefest nod.

All Merlin pulls out is a thick envelope. "Ulfric's
retiring. I'm taking over as president. The club voted to
give this to Rock. You know, help cover some of his
troubles. And thank you for keeping quiet."

Wrath snaps the envelope out of Merlin's hand. "We
don't snitch."

"I know. Didn't mean any disrespect." Merlin hesitates
and glances at Whisper, then back at Wrath. "So, we're
good?"

"Yeah. Where'd Ulfric retire to?"

"He's still alive, if that's what you're asking," Whisper
answers. "He moved down to South Carolina to be near
some family."

He may have gotten careless in his old age, but Ulfric
has always been a decent guy, so that's good news.

We discuss a few more minor issues. As instructed by
Rock this morning in church, Wrath never mentions any

of the changes going on in Ironworks. The Wolf Knights seem to have no clue that we've teamed up with the Green Street Crew to dismantle the Vipers MC and take over their territory. There was a time when we would have called on Ulfric to help us out and split the territory with them. But the Wolf Knights have proved to be unreliable in a few recent matters. I wonder if this will impact Wrath's relationship with Whisper in the future. As far as I know, they've always kept the gym they own separate from club business. It's really none of *my* business, so I push the thought out of my head.

On our way back, I'm struck by the view of the party from the distance. "Trin did a really nice job on all this."

Wrath turns and grins at me. "Good practice for the next one."

I'm so stuck in my own head and my own issues that at first I assume he means Heidi and Axel. It takes a second to realize he means Trinity and him. "Yeah? That happening?"

He's not even annoyed by the question. "Fuck yeah, it is." Before we walk back into the tent, he stops me with a hand on my arm. "I know you got Serena here, but I still have business to take care of. Will you look out for Trin?" He tilts his head at Sway and his crew. I don't need any more information from Wrath.

"You know it."

Rock catches my eye and raises his eyebrow. The expression has the same effect on me it did when I was twelve. I've never *feared* Rock, but I never want to disappoint him either. Next to me, Wrath snickers. "Here," he says, pulling the envelope Whisper gave him out of his pocket. "I'll let you take care of this."

"Gee, thanks."

I make my way up front and hate like hell that I'm intruding because now our prez and first lady are busy making fuck-me eyes at each other. *Jesus Christ.*

I clear my throat and drop into the chair on Rock's other side. Rock's all business as he turns and meets my eyes. I lean in and lower my voice. "All taken care of. Ulfric's enjoying retirement down south and Merlin took his place at the head of the table."

Prez rolls his eyes. "Great. He's about as sharp as a tire."

"They didn't even ask about Ironworks," I say, lowering my voice even more.

"Good. Not their concern."

I slip the envelope out of my cut and hand it over to Rock. He takes a quick peek inside and passes it back to me. "That's for you," I protest. "From Merlin. For the trouble—"

"Whole club went through hell," Rock states with a bland expression.

"You were in *jail*." My whisper comes out a little harsher than I meant it to, but Rock's not offended.

The corner of his mouth quirks up. "I'm aware." He searches the crowd but doesn't seem to find who he wants. "Have Teller put it in the safe. We'll deal with it tomorrow," he orders not leaving any room for discussion.

That's Rock, though. He had three months of his life stolen, but his first concern is still the club…our family.

Never himself. My gaze flicks to Hope. At least now Rock has someone to take care of *him* for a change.

My chest squeezes as Heidi sneaks up behind Hope and hugs her. They talk for a while. Nothing I'm able to overhear. Not until the end, when she announces she's leaving to go for a ride with Axel. I restrain myself. What am I supposed to do—cause a scene? Not with Rock smirking at me like he knows exactly what's going on in my head.

Heidi eventually stands, leaving Hope's side and hugs Rock. "Congratulations, Uncle Rock. Thank you…thank you for everything," she says so low, I almost can't hear her.

"Love you, Heidi-girl."

Her eyes tear up, but she kisses his cheek. Her gaze briefly meets mine and before she leaves she gives me a sad smile that I'm not sure how to interpret.

Heidi

FROM YEARS of visiting my brother at the clubhouse, I know my way around the woods fairly well. Well enough, that I know when Axel takes my hand and leads me out of the tent, we're not headed to the clubhouse.

"What are you doing?"

"I want to be alone with you and I know we'll be bothered at the clubhouse."

My mouth tugs into a smile, and I let him lead me into the trees. Abruptly he stops and pulls me against him. It's so dark, I can barely see. But I feel the heat of him against me. Feel his mouth brush against my forehead.

"Thought you wanted to go for a ride?" I ask softly.

"Oh, I want to give you a ride."

Laughter spills out of me, and I poke him in the side, wiggling my fingers until he laughs. "Come on. I want to change. I don't want to ruin my dress. And I'm uncomfortable."

He sighs and takes my hand, this time leading us to the clubhouse.

Outside we find my brother and Mariella, sitting so close, they're touching from shoulder to leg. "Aww," I mutter under my breath. I really like Mariella. I think she's good for my brother. I can't tell if they're friends or something more, but she's sweet and quiet. She seems to have calmed him somewhat in the short time she's been here. She's certainly diverted his attention from hovering over me so much, which I'm grateful for.

"Hi, Marcel," I call out. Next to me, Axel groans, but I ignore him and run over to hug my brother.

"Where you headed, baby sis?" he asks, keeping his arm around my waist.

"Upstairs. I want to change, and then we're going to go for a ride." I tense, waiting for my brother to say *no fucking way* or something equally big-brotherly-obnoxious.

His jaw tightens, but he nods. Looking past me, he fixes his scary big-brother face on Axel. "Take it easy with her on the back of your bike."

"Of course, I will," Axel answers respectfully, then adds, "I always do," a little less respectfully. Marcel drills him with a stare and Axel fidgets.

Exasperated, I grab Axel's hand, dragging him away. "Come on."

Safely inside my room, I flip the lock just in case my brother decides to check up on us. Axel takes it differently, pressing his body against my back until my cheek's resting against the door. "What are you doing?" I ask.

Warm breath skates over my shoulders, then rough fingers trace down my back. "Helping you out of your dress."

"Oh," soft laughter flows out of me, then a shiver as he pulls his weight away. His hands find my zipper, tugging it down. The dress falls at my feet, and I lean over to pick it up.

"Heidi," Axel says in a low, rough voice that makes my insides dance.

Voices from downstairs reach us and my body tenses. While the brothers treat the clubhouse as their own personal sex club, for Axel and I to fool around here is playing with fire. Anyone who overhears us is likely to go tattle to my brother. "Not here, Axel."

He groans. "You always gonna be his slave?"

Confused I turn and face him. "Who?"

"You know who."

"God, not this again," I snap, pushing past him to hang the dress up in my closet. I grab a pair of folded up jeans, flick them open and hop into them. I'm so tired of fighting about my friendship with Murphy. Since Axel's a prospect for the club, I'm sure his interaction with Murphy isn't always fun—the guys love to hassle the prospects—but he's been a huge part of my life *forever*.

Axel has to understand he's like another brother to me. That's all.

Keep telling yourself that, Heidi.

I grew out of my little-girl crush on Blake years ago.

Sure you did.

Reaching up on tiptoes, I grab a T-shirt and slip it on.

"Tell me I'm wrong about Murphy."

"You're wrong," I fire back.

"Okay," Axel says, sounding anything but okay.

When I turn, he's sitting on my bed staring at me. I grab my cosmetic case and hairbrush from the top of my dresser and wiggle them in my hand. "I'll be right back."

A smile flickers over his mouth, then he gestures at the door in a "hurry up" motion.

Because I'm not a member, my room doesn't have an attached bathroom like the ones at the opposite end of the hallway do. I'm not complaining, though. I'm so thrilled I'm allowed to stay up here from time to time, they could make me sleep in the kitchen and I'd happily roll out a sleeping bag in the pantry.

It takes longer than I expected to work all the bobby pins out of my hair. I should have asked Axel to help me. Flipping my hair over, one more bobby pin clatters on the tile floor. I snatch it up and set it with the rest of them, then brush my teeth. The bathroom is dorm-style and unisex. I'm not worried about someone intruding on me. I don't even bother looking up when the door opens. The click of the lock grabs my attention though.

I spit out the foamy ball of toothpaste, rinse my mouth, and turn. "Murphy? What are you doing?"

He doesn't move closer, just watches me for a few

seconds. "Wanted to check on you. Make sure you're okay."

Taking a closer look, I notice he's holding an icepack over one of his hands. "Oh my God, what happened?" I ask, rushing over.

The corners of his mouth turn up slightly. "I'm fine. It's nothing."

Skeptical, my lips slide into a smirk. "Were you guys just messing around or is it something more serious?"

He gives me a harder look. "It's nothing." Shifting slightly, he sets the icepack on the counter and reaches out to brush my hair back from my face. "You took your hair down."

My skin tingles where his fingers brushed against me. "Yeah," I answer with a nervous tremor in my voice. My hands flail in the air around my head. "All the bobby pins. So tight…it was giving me a headache." Why am I so flustered?

"It looks pretty down."

"Thank you." Nervously, I grab a ponytail holder from my pocket and start twisting my hair into a braid. It's all lumpy and snarled from the up-do, though, so it comes out messy. "Damn," I mutter, yanking it back out.

"Here, let me help," Blake offers, steering me to the mirror. He picks up my brush and gently tugs out all the knots, brushing my hair until it's smooth. Blake used to do this for me all the time when I was a kid, but it's…been a while.

"Do you still remember how to braid?" I whisper.

I'm watching him in the mirror, so I see the way his

mouth slides into a warm smile. "Yeah, I remember. You got a pink bow you want me to stick in it?"

"No." I bump him with my elbow for teasing me.

He works slowly, gathering all my hair in his hands. The tug and pull as he twists my hair into a loose braid soothes me and brings back a lot of memories. My eyes squeeze shut and I let myself enjoy the simple moment. When he reaches the end, he secures the braid with an elastic I hand him.

"You two going for a ride?" he asks quietly.

His low voice seeps into my mind, nudging me out of my trance. "Yeah. It's a pretty night."

He nods and stuffs his hands in his pockets.

"What's wrong?" I ask, turning around.

"Nothing. Be careful."

"We will."

He still doesn't move. "Anything else?"

Finally he meets my gaze. "Yeah. I'm uh, gonna be out of town for a bit. Some club stuff. But I'll be back for your birthday."

My eighteenth birthday is in a few weeks. Blake's never missed a single one of my birthdays. Something soft and warm wraps itself around my heart. He didn't want me to think he was abandoning me. "Going anywhere interesting?" I ask.

"Not really." He flicks his gaze up. "I'll take you for your birthday ride, and maybe we can do something fun?"

"Okay. Like what?"

His mouth slides into a smirk and he runs his hand over his beard. "We can go apple picking."

I snort, then giggle, and he smiles even wider. "We haven't done that in years."

"No," he agrees.

"I think Trinity said something about having a small birthday party up here for me."

"So, we'll go before the party or the next day."

"Where?"

"Picking Ladder Farm?"

"Okay. I'd like that."

He hesitates, then leans in and presses the softest kiss to my cheek.

"See you then," he says before turning and walking out the door.

ZERO

Lilly

"DON'T BE MAD, but I'm driving behind a really pretty girl."

"What?" I ask.

Z repeats the bizarre statement.

"Did you really call me to tell me you're out picking up chicks on my best friend's wedding day?"

His laughter comes through the line low and rich. If he were in front of me, I'd kick him.

"I'm driving behind *you*."

"Oh." My gaze flicks to the rear view mirror, but all I see is a big, black SUV. "Figures that's what you'd drive. It looks like an undercover FBI vehicle."

He chuckles again and this time his laughter melts me like butter. "It's Rock's."

"What are you doing?"

"I needed to run an errand for him. What are *you* doing? I thought you stayed with Hope and Trin last night?"

"I did." Z had been pretty annoyed I didn't sneak out and come stay with *him*. But for once in my life, I chose girlfriends over dick. I didn't regret it either. "I needed to run out for a topcoat."

"What?"

"Nail polish. For the bride."

"Ohhhkay."

"Shut up."

"Let me get ahead of you, so I can open the gate."

I pull my car slightly to the right and he zips around me, flipping his blinker on and turning onto what barely looks like a road. It's a good thing he found me because I'm not sure I would have remembered to turn here.

It isn't the first time I've wondered about all the secrecy surrounding the Lost Kings MC. Z's usually tight-lipped about anything related to the club. Not that I ask a lot of questions. Or that we do a lot of talking.

But now that one of my best friends is marrying into the club, I'm curious. Hope is a lawyer. And based on the multiple warnings my brother has given me to stay away from Z, the Lost Kings are criminals.

Alexander—what I call my brother when he's busy lecturing me on how to live my life, because it annoys him when I use his full name—doesn't understand that Rock treats Hope like a fucking queen. It's hard not to be intrigued.

I don't want that. I don't need a man in my life permanently. Just in my bed from time to time. Z has been all too willing to offer those services on what's becoming a regular basis.

I park a little way down the driveway—in case I want to leave early. Z parks next to me and opens my car door before I have a chance to grab my bag and purse.

"Why'd you park all the way down here?"

"I didn't want to get blocked in if I need to run out again."

He gives me a skeptical look, as if he's not buying my bullshit. Before I explain further, he extends his hand and I swear to the big stone Buddha statue at the bottom of the hill, I want to swoon. And I'm not a swooner.

A few seconds later, I want to do something else.

Z shuts my door, then presses me up against it with his big bulky body. "You have any idea what it did to me last night? Having you under the same roof but not being able to touch you?"

The minute his body brushes against mine, any self-restraint I'd been holding on to flies away in the sweet autumn breeze.

Zero

LILLY'S beautiful eyes widen but her body melts against mine. "Tell me," she says in the same husky tone she uses after we fuck.

Rock expressed a strong preference that I not bother the girls last night. Since he's the groom, and my president, I didn't.

"It made me crazy." That's not a lie, either. It's been way too long since I've had Lilly. Knowing she was here last night under the same roof, and I couldn't have her, made me half-crazed with lust.

Tonight's another story.

The happy couple will be enjoying their wedded bliss, and I'll be enjoying Lilly.

"I forgot the stuff I ran out to get. Fuck," she mutters, pushing away from me and opening the door.

Inside, I'm groaning. The way her luscious mouth spits out the word *fuck* is incredibly hot. Reminds me of the way she says it when she's riding my dick.

I need to make that happen again.

Soon.

Like right now. Because having Lilly bent over in front of me while she stretches across the front seat to grab her tiny plastic bag seriously tests my restraint. It's a battle with my inner horndog not to fit my hands over her perfectly curved hips, yank her pants down and slam into her.

I'm hard just picturing it.

She backs out of the car, bumping right into my groin, and pure instinct makes me put my hands on her hips. "Sorry," she says, straightening up.

My hands stay where they are. I close the car door and this time press her front to the car, fitting myself against her back. Lifting her thick, heavy hair up, I push it over one shoulder. My lips find her neck and my hips grind against her ass—just enough to tease her.

"Z, what are you doing?" She can barely get the words out.

"Preview of what's going down later."

"Oh, really?" she says in her teasing way. "I thought weddings were great for meeting chicks."

Slowly, I inch back and turn her to face me. "You're the only chick I want. And we've already met. Several times."

She snorts, and I fit my fingers under her chin, lifting her head so she meets my eyes. "I'm not feeding you bullshit, Lilly."

Doesn't she get it by now?

"What if I wasn't in the wedding party?"

"Then you would've been my plus one."

She drops a little bit of her prickly wall, and leans into me, brushing a soft kiss on my cheek. Before she pulls away, I lift my hands to either side of her head, holding her still so I can kiss her deeper, really taking my time to remind her of all the ways our bodies fit perfectly together.

A soft moan flows out of her mouth and into mine and her hands go to my waistband, yanking me closer.

"Something to think about," I say when we part.

"I'll be thinking about it," she whispers.

Instead of pushing her into the woods, tearing off her clothes, and fucking her up against a tree, I take Lilly's hand and lead her up the driveway.

There's a wedding to get ready for.

Inside the clubhouse, I reluctantly let go of Lilly's

hand. After yanking her to me for one last kiss. "See you in a bit."

Her cheeks turn a bit pink, which is cute on Lilly. Few things embarrass her.

Like a lovesick pup, I watch her until she stops at Trinity's door.

Sparky and Stash are hanging out in the living room rolling joints. "Party favors," Sparky says, then falls over into a fit of giggles.

"Good to see you're ready for the wedding," I bite out. They ignore my sarcasm and keep rolling.

"Idiots," I mutter.

"I heard that," Sparky yells as I run up the stairs. Ignoring the stoner twins, I stride down the hallway and knock on Rock's door. Well, after tonight it won't be his room anymore. He and Hope are finally moving into their house. If I were sentimental, I might have some words about that.

Okay, I'm a little sentimental. It's the end of an era.

Am I jealous?

Maybe.

Rock's standing in front of his dresser fixing he knot in his tie. I flick my gaze at Wrath, positive it's killing him not to poke fun at our best friend for the suit and tie. His mouth turns up in a grin. Twenty bucks says he's already ribbed Rock about the suit.

"Ready?" I ask Rock.

"Fuck yes." His eyes meet mine, and I sense the briefest hesitation in them. "She's still here, right?"

"Oh, Christ," Wrath mutters. "Cinderella isn't going anywhere."

"Nah, I made sure I locked the front gate after me," I add helpfully.

"Thanks, asshole," Rock growls.

Satisfied or fed up with the tie, Rock drops his hands and turns away from the mirror. "What'd Loco want?"

"Oh." Yeah, meeting up with Lilly had wiped my brain clean of the whole reason I went out in the first place. I yank an envelope out of my pocket and hand it to Rock. "Wedding present. I think he was insulted he didn't get an invite."

"For fuck's sake," he curses under his breath, grabbing the envelope and setting it on the dresser without opening it. "With the crews we have coming in, that's all we would have needed."

Imagining that scenario makes me laugh and Rock glares at me. "What? Come on, that'd be some funny shit."

"More like Loco would be trying to make deals with everyone behind our backs," Wrath says.

Rock doesn't even turn around. "Exactly."

"He's already got something set up with Sway."

"Yeah, can you imagine him trying to work a deal with Stump?" Wrath's mouth curls into a smirk. "That old bastard would probably shoot Loco." He chuckles as if he's reconsidering inviting Loco up.

"I don't want anything going wrong today." Rock's so damn tense. When he's not looking, I make a *what the fuck* face at Wrath.

"Hope imposed a no sex before the wedding thing on him," Wrath explains.

Rock glares at him. "Shut up."

Well, that explains it. I take a more serious look at my

best friend. I've known Rock since we were teenagers. Was there for his first shitshow of a marriage.

"You did good, prez. She's a keeper," I say to reassure him. Just in case.

He responds with a brief smile. "Don't I know it."

The three of us have been friends for a long damn time. Before the club. And we love to joke around, razz each other, and generally act like obnoxious fucks. But Rock turns to both of us with a serious expression. "Thank you for everything. I know I'm throwing a lot on both of you today—"

Wrath isn't one for all the feel-good shit. "Anything you need. You know that, brother."

Rock's phone buzzes. Thank fuck. For a second I thought we were all going to kick back and pluck our eyebrows together.

"Shit," Rock grumbles, looking at his phone. "It's Damon. Can you go meet them down the road and show them the way here?"

Eager to get out of here, I'm saying yes before he even finishes the sentence. Wrath stands to join me, but I stop him. "I got it, bro."

He flips me off. Happy to have something useful to do, I hustle out the door.

Lilly

"I'M BACK," I call out as I enter Trinity's room waving the bottle of topcoat in the air.

"Thank God," Trinity says, rushing over to take the bottle out of my hand.

No one asks why I took so damn long. Good thing, because I'm too busy reliving my moments with Z. He seemed different somehow today. Do guys get fluttery romantic feelings at weddings the way some women do?

Guys like Z? Doubt it.

I certainly don't.

I'm thrilled for Hope, but I'm not standing here mentally picking out flowers and designing a wedding dress.

While Trinity paints Hope's nails, I duck into the bathroom to slip into my bridesmaid dress. Hope's been a fun, un-fussy bride. She let us pick out whatever we wanted, didn't expect elaborate parties, or any other bridezilla nonsense. The wedding really is about the two of them and their love for each other. Even someone as jaded as I am finds it sweet.

Once I've secured my boobs and zipped my dress, I step out in time to watch Trinity fix Hope's hair.

We indulge in a lot of pre-wedding banter until it's time for Z to come collect us.

Other than trading in his jeans for a pair of gray cargo pants, he looks the same as always.

"You didn't dress up for the wedding?" I tease as I follow the girls outside.

"Sure I did." He grins, pointing to his pants and flashing dimples.

Z's drives Hope, Trinity and me to the wedding site. Heidi's with Murphy. Teller gets Mara. When Hope first explained the wedding was happening at the clubhouse, I thought she was nuts. But as we maneuver through the woods in the UTV, I understand why. It's beautiful.

I can't imagine the trouble Trinity must have gone to setting this up. Guilt simmers over me for not being a better bridesmaid.

We park and Z helps Hope out. She and Rock meet and, well, they're in their own little world. Wrath meets Trinity and asks where Heidi and Murphy are. Somehow we lost them along the way.

Z walks up and offers me his hand. "Hey, pretty girl." His low, smooth voice does all sort of inappropriate things to my insides.

My voice fails me, and I realize I'm staring at him like an idiot. Finally, I reach out and take his hand, and a jolt of awareness heats my body.

He sort of dips his head, almost like a shy gesture. Z's anything but shy, so I'm intrigued. "You're...that color's beautiful on you. You look amazing."

His words come out so serious that again, I'm at a loss for words.

"Were you guys drinking this morning?" he asks as we join the others.

"No. Why?"

"You seem off." He leans in close to whisper in my ear, "And because I need you fully sober for all the things I plan to do to you when this is over."

Our eyes meet and he winks.

He takes his place across the aisle from me, leaning over to say something in Wrath's ear. The big blond chuckles softly and nods.

Zero

"Twenty dollars says they're fucking before this thing's over," I say to Wrath in a low voice when I join him on Rock's side of the aisle.

He shakes with laughter and nods, but doesn't respond. He's too fixated on watching Trinity. Probably thinking about what kind of wedding Trinity will arrange for them.

My gaze drifts to Lilly. Fuck, she ripped the air right out of my lungs when I saw her this morning. She's prickly, though. Probably have to *trick* her into marrying me.

The ceremony's over quick. Boxes of butterflies are passed around, and everyone releases them into the air.

I've really had my fill of all this girly shit. But based on what I've seen some of my cousins go through with their wives, I suppose it could have been a lot worse. Rock's a lucky bastard.

Would Lilly be some crazed bride trying to micro-manage everything down to my underwear? Or would she be happy with something simple like this?

I doubt I'll ever know.

Shit. In the last few months, I've watched the two people in the world closest to me voluntarily settle down. It leaves me coming up with a lot of stupid ideas.

Unfortunately, the only girl on my mind these days is Lilly. Even though she'll dodge me for weeks at a time, I still can't get enough of her. The amount of fucks I should give that I have to chase after her are hard to come up with.

Lilly

"YOU THINK ABOUT GETTIN' married?" Z asks as he watches Rock feed Hope a bite of cake.

The wedding was beautiful. Food has been amazing. Poor Trinity's been running around all night.

And Z's asking me if I think about marriage? "God, no," I finally answer.

"Never?"

A catch in his voice makes me turn my head. "*You* do?"

"Yeah," he states matter-of-factly.

"Why?"

He stares at me as if a flock of butterflies just flew out of my mouth instead of a one-word question. "Same reason anyone does." He nods at Rock and Hope, who are so immersed in each other it almost feels like an invasion of privacy to watch them.

"I don't think everyone who gets married has what they have," I say as I turn back toward Z.

"No. Probably not."

While I admire my friend for sticking by her man while he went through some trouble this summer, I know for a fact I couldn't do it. Visit Z in jail? No way. It would break me. Not to mention how horrified my family would be. It's not like I can't guess that Z's motorcycle club is more than a club. That they're into some shady stuff. Maybe Hope managed to convince herself of her husband's innocence, but since meeting Z, I've heard enough stories about the Lost Kings MC to know that they're anything but innocent. While Z's hot, great in bed, and super sweet, he's not marriage material.

I don't think explaining any of that at his best friend's wedding is the polite thing to do, so I force a smile instead.

Besides, I wasn't lying. The last thing I want to do is get married. Let any man think he owns me. And a guy like Z would definitely be the *I-own-you-caveman-type* of husband.

Fuck that.

"Marriage is for suckers," the guy across from us says, slurring each word. He has the nerve to jab a ham-sized finger in the air at me. "She's hot now, but give her ten years. She'll be fat and do nothing but bitch at ya."

Z leans over the table, grabbing the guy by his shirt. "Watch your fuckin' mouth, asshole." He growls a few more warnings so low, I can't hear them. The guy ends up shuffling away after flipping Z off.

"Sorry," he mutters as he sits back down.

"One of your brothers?" It's hard to keep the sarcasm out of my voice.

"Sort of. He's from another charter and he's a dick. No one here would ever think something like that, let alone say it."

It's true. None of the guys I've met before have ever been rude. Slightly terrifying, yes. Rude, no.

Trinity breezes by and drops into the chair next to me. "Are you having fun?" she asks breathlessly.

"Are *you*? You've been running non-stop all day."

She waves off my concern. "I'm done for the night."

"Sure you are," I tease.

Trinity's boyfriend…no there's nothing *boy* about him. Trinity's *man* lumbers over, settling a hand on her shoulder. They stare at each other with complete adoration for a few seconds, before he lifts his chin at Z.

The two guys do this unspoken conversation thing, that's actually fascinating to watch. Next thing I know, Z's sliding his chair back.

"I need to take care of something. You okay?"

"Sure, as long as that guy doesn't come back."

Z's gaze searches the tent. "If anyone bothers you"—he points out two guys with Lost Kings MC cuts on—"let Dex or Ravage know." He shifts and I follow his line of sight. "You know Murphy and Teller. They'll look out for you, too."

"Uh, okay."

"I'll take care of her, Z. Go ahead," Trinity says. She pokes Wrath in the side. "Go do what you need to so you can hurry back." He flashes a smile so warm he almost doesn't look so scary. After they're gone, she raises an eyebrow at me. "Someone bother you?"

"Not really." I don't want to seem like I'm complaining. I've dealt with plenty of rude, drunk men in my life. I can handle it. "So you really went with a monarch theme," I tease, nodding at the table at the head of the room where the bride and groom are.

Tittering laughter bubbles out of her. "Yeah. The whole king and queen thing. That's what we do here."

A young woman slides into the seat across from us. "Hey," she greets.

Trinity flashes a tight smile at the girl. "How's it going, Sasha?"

"This is really something."

"Is it your first LOKI wedding?"

"Yes." The girl swings her vacant gaze my way. "Whose old lady are you?"

"Uh," I glance at Trinity unsure how to answer the question. From spending time with Z and listening to Hope, I know what an old lady is. Well, I know enough to know that's not what I am to Z.

"She's with our VP," Trinity answers for me.

"Oh."

"Who are you with?" I ask to be friendly.

She lifts a lazy finger, pointing across the room at a cluster of guys with cuts claiming a different territory than Z's. "Crazyhorse. I ain't his old lady, though. Well—" she giggles. "I am at club events. His wife's one-hundred percent citizen."

I'm not sure how to respond to that. I glance at Trinity whose staring daggers at the girl. Before she responds, someone calls her away. "I'll be right back."

Leaning forward, I catch Sasha's attention. "Forgive me, but what did you mean about citizen?" I ask, because hell, I'm curious.

"Oh. You know. She's like his wife outside the club. Like, legal wife. Raises his kids, takes care of the house. But when he's with me, it's all just fun, you know?"

"And she knows about you?"

She gives me a sly grin. "I'm sure she does."

"And you're okay just being his piece of ass?"

She snorts, not insulted—not that I care if she is. "Yeah. I get to do the fun stuff with him. All bikers are like that. They all date you know, like, girls *my* age," she says, as if she wants to really make sure I understand that I'm an old hag or something.

"That's fascinating." She doesn't even blink at the caustic tone of my voice.

"So you're new to the life, then? Like her?" She jerks her thumb in Hope's direction. "She's so fucking stuck-up."

This chick realizes I was in the wedding, right? "She's actually one of my best friends. And she's as far from stuck-up as a person can get."

"Oh." Her lips quiver into a smile. "Sorry. I haven't, uh really talked to her much."

"Then maybe you shouldn't run your mouth about stuff you know nothing about?"

"Whatever." She stands and storms off.

I guess I got a pretty good dose of reality tonight. If I ever thought about Z and I being something more permanent—which I don't—I'd have to put up with him having club girls on the side while I sit home pretending I didn't know what he was up to.

Double fuck that.

No. What we have is perfect. What we have is all we'll ever be.

I don't recognize the guys at the table next to us. But they're wearing Lost Kings MC cuts like Z's. Their bottom rockers claim downstate New York as their territory. One loud, drunk one catches my attention. He aims his glare at Murphy, who's up front talking to Rock. "That fuck is so far up her ass ain't even funny. You believe none of them were fuckin' her while he was inside?"

A round of drunk noises of disbelief go around the table. Are they talking about Hope? I lean back in my chair a little further, straining to catch more of their conversation without appearing obvious.

"Sorry," Trinity says setting her hand on my shoulder and dropping into the chair next to me.

My face must betray the eavesdropping I was attempting. "Everything okay?" she asks.

"Oh, yeah. Who are those guys? The loud one?" I tip my head toward the "downstate" table.

"That's the president of our downstate charter." Her eyes narrow as she studies my face. "He didn't bother you, did he?"

"No. Nothing like that."

"Okay. Z should be back any second."

Right after she says it, her man strides back into the tent. He takes a seat next to her and pulls her into his lap.

Now, where is Z?

As if my body's aware of his every movement, my gaze lands on him coming in the back of the tent.

He searches the crowd and when his eyes meet mine, his mouth curves into a wide smile.

It really sucks that he's so fucking gorgeous, he makes my knees weak every time he flashes his dimples my way.

Zero

"WHAT THE FUCK DOES STUMP WANT?" I grumble at Wrath once we're away from the wedding tent.

"How the fuck should I know?" he grumbles right back. "I have my own things to take care of tonight."

I slap his arm with the back of my hand. "Care to share?"

"No."

The clubhouse will be too packed for discussing business. We head down to the stone amphitheater where the wedding was held. Any meetings we needed to have with visiting MCs tonight would happen out here. Wrath and Murphy have the honor of dealing with the Wolf Knight sit-down. Wrath and I get to deal with the Devil Demon's president, Stump.

Stump's actually not a bad guy. He's old as fuck, though. His son Chaser should really be running things by now, but Stump isn't giving up control of his club any time soon. Chaser is the VP and he's sitting in on this meeting as well.

"Can't believe your prez went through with that," Stump says after we get greetings out of the way.

Like the half-caveman he is, Wrath grunts. "She's a good girl."

"Where we at on my supply?" Stump asks.

Wrath answers that question. "We're still tight. Demand's high. We have certain people aware of our connection, so you might want to look into that."

Stump cocks his head to the side. "Maybe the leak's on your end."

"Unlikely," I answer.

Father and son share a look, but don't comment further. As if they're already aware there might be a problem in their crew.

Not my business.

To keep the peace, I offer up a small quantity that the club agreed to ahead of time. "Sparky set aside an O for you to take home."

Stump aims a pissed-off biker expression my way. An ounce is way under the quantity the Demons were looking to purchase.

"On the house," Wrath adds. "It's a new strain Sparky cultivated. Slightly higher THC count."

Stump's irritation disappears. Who can be mad about free weed? Especially the quality shit we're known for growing.

"Appreciate that," he says.

Thank fuck for Sparky and his miracle green thumbs. "Just talk to Sparky or Stash before you leave."

"Anything else?" Wrath asks. He's calm and controlled. Only because I know him so well is it obvious that he's itching to get this over with.

While Stump's a decent guy, he's also a talker. Something Wrath doesn't have a whole lot of patience for. Honestly, I don't have much patience for it either since I want to get back to Lilly.

Stump's face pulls into a mask of seriousness. "I have a request."

"Actually, *I* do," Chaser says. "My son, Dylan. He's gonna be at Empire State next semester. I'm—"

"You want us to look out for him?" I ask.

"Kind of. He's a good kid. Not a lot of trouble." He nods at Wrath. "He's been in MMA since—"

"Since his sister pelted him in the ass with her BB gun,"

Stump interrupts with a laugh. "That's how he got tagged with Target."

"Good road name." I snicker.

Chaser sighs and runs his hand over his chin. "Yeah."

Wrath actually cracks a smile. "The sister's not coming too, is she?"

Stump glares at Wrath for asking about his granddaughter, even though we all know Wrath didn't mean anything by it. "Fuck no. She ain't—"

"Anyway," Chaser says, interrupting his father. "He'd like to train with you." He nods at Wrath.

"He can come into Furious whenever. No problem," Wrath says. He does *not* say anything about having the kid up to the clubhouse.

"He ride?" I ask.

The old man's face pulls down in disgust, while Chaser rolls his eyes. "Fuckin' rice burner," Stump spits out.

Next to me, Wrath's choking down his laughter. Obviously, his grandson's choice of bike is killing Stump.

Chaser shrugs. "He bought it with his own money."

"I'll still let him train at Furious," Wrath says, barely keeping the grin off his face.

"We've had trouble with the Viper charter trying to push up from Pennsylvania. Just in case. Want to make sure he's protected."

"He living on campus?" I ask.

Chaser shrugs. "Think so. Haven't ironed it all out yet."

"You got our numbers. Let us know what you need. We'll keep an eye on him." Wrath gives me a look, like he's not interested in babysitting some other club's kid. But we have a long history with the Demons. Helping them out isn't a big hardship and earns us a favor down the road.

Lilly

"MISS ME?" Z asks, leaning over the back of my chair. His fingertips brush over my bare shoulder, setting off sparks of desire.

"Actually, yes." Why lie?

He pulls me out of my chair, making Trinity laugh. His hands fit over my hips, yanking me close to dance for a few songs. Every press of his body against mine makes me wish we were alone.

After Hope and Rock make their exit—and Z made it clear he expects me to stay over—I'm ready to rip his clothes off and have my way with him in the woods if need be.

"You've got a lot of pretty girls here. Sure you want me to stick around?"

He pulls back, and I want shove the words back into my mouth. I'm never so insecure around a guy. Tonight I'm rattled, for lots of reasons.

"Yeah, Lilly. I want you to stick around," he says so seriously, my heart thumps.

"Are you drunk?" I ask.

"Not at all," he answers in a tone of voice that's almost grave.

I don't need a whole lot of convincing. Although staying at the clubhouse reminds me an awful lot of sleeping at a frat house, I'm not sure where else we'd go at this hour.

"Heading out?" the big scary blond one asks with a smirk. Z punches him in the arm and he barely reacts, except to laugh.

"Do you need me?" Z asks, dropping the attitude.

"Nah, we're good. I'm going to head back in a few minutes myself."

The glow from the wedding site only carries so far, but Z seems very sure of where he's going. He does take my hand, though. "Sorry, all the UTVs are being used, or I would drive us back."

"It's fine. It's pretty at night." It is too. Except for the party going on behind us, it's peaceful…tranquil up here. I can see why Z likes it so much.

A couple of guys are in the yard in front of the clubhouse. Z doesn't stop to talk to any of them.

"In a hurry?" I tease.

"Yeah. Don't want you to change your mind."

"Hey." I stop and yank on his hand until he looks at me. "I'm not leaving."

He flashes a quick smile, dimples and all, then leans in until we're so close, I can taste the sweet mint on his breath.

"You want me, pretty girl?"

I lose myself in his clear blue eyes. Endless midnight blue like a cold winter night sky. "I always want you."

He closes the distance and our lips meet. Slow at first. For a rough guy, Z can be awfully gentle when he wants to be. Then his fingers grip my ass, pulling me closer. My mouth opens and he slides his tongue inside, stroking softly.

Someone whistles at us, and he pulls away. I duck my head, not sure why I'm embarrassed. Z doesn't bother answering the catcall. Instead, he leads me into the clubhouse. Except for two guys and a girl in the living room, the downstairs is deserted.

"Give me a second?" Z asks.

I nod, and he pulls me over to the couch. "Hey, Willow." He nods at the girl, and she smiles back.

Jealousy sinks its dirty claws into my skin. Who is she? How do they know each other? Maybe Z senses the change in me. He squeezes my hand and pulls me closer. "Lilly, this is Willow. She tends bar for us down at Crystal Ball. Willow, this is my girl, Lilly." He doesn't look at me or stumble over the words *my girl*.

I don't know how I feel about that. I'm a grown-ass woman. I should be insulted. But I kind of like Z introducing me as his girl.

Willow nods and gives me a warm smile while Z continues introducing me to his brothers, Sparky and Stash.

"Interesting road names, guys."

Sparky grins but doesn't offer a story behind his name.

Niceties over with, Z gets down to business. "Stump's gonna stop by later for—"

Sparky cuts him off with a serene smile and quick, "Got it."

Z nods and takes me upstairs.

Briefly, I wonder which one of the scary guys at the wedding was named Stump and what he's stopping by for.

"You need me to watch the dogs, brother?" Sparky asks with a quick glance at me.

Z grins. "Yeah. You mind?"

"Nope."

Sparky follows us upstairs and when Z opens his door, two pups wriggle out, dancing and pawing at Z's legs.

"Down," he orders them.

"Oh my God, they're so sweet," I squeal like a little girl. Squatting down, I take a few minutes to pet them. "Hope mentioned the dogs. I didn't realize they were yours." I tilt my head so I can see Z's face.

He shrugs. "They're the club's dogs, but I'm training them."

Sparky lets a short sharp whistle loose and the pups snap to attention.

"Looks like they answer to him too." I chuckle.

Z's not one of those guys who feels his manhood's been threatened when his dogs listen to someone else. "It's good for them to be used to other people."

They follow Sparky back downstairs. "Don't get them high," Z shouts after him. Sparky's laughter is the only answer we get.

Fun time's over. Z's face is almost ferocious as he nudges me into his room and shuts the door. He wraps his arms around me, pushing my back against the wall. "Eager much?" I tease.

"Fuck yeah. I don't think you understand what you do to me, Lilly."

Yes, I do because I feel the same way. Z takes my hand and kisses my fingertips. There's something about this big, beautiful, tattooed and dimpled man that makes my heart kick up every damn time he focuses his attention on me. Warmth rushes through my veins. Tingles race up and down my spine. He's the only one who's ever had this effect on me.

His blue eyes bore into mine, shining with lust and need. Need that hits me right between my thighs. My body always reacts this way to Z whether I want it to or not.

Good thing I want it. Want *him*. Bad.

"Do you want me to fuck you, Lilly?" he asks with his serious expression in place.

"Yes." I don't bother hesitating or doing the hard-to-get thing. Z would see right through it anyway.

Tipping my head to the side, I take in his room.

"You've been here before," he reminds me.

Yes, except I'd come in tipsy with him in the middle of the night. We'd gotten off, slept for a few hours and I took off before sunrise.

He steps back, and lets his gaze roam over my body.

"Is black your favorite color?" I ask, nodding at the bed with its black comforter and sheets. The furniture's all black lacquer too.

His lips quirk up. "And red."

"Aren't your club's colors blue and gray?"

He cocks his head. "You know my club's colors?"

"Well." I hedge. "It's hard not to."

He lifts a hand, tracing a finger over my collarbone and down to the keyhole opening in my dress. "Did you know red was my favorite color?"

"No. It just looks really good on me."

"Fuckin' A it does."

"So you don't like blue and gray?"

He seems confused by the question. Hell, I'm not even sure why I asked myself.

"It's not about that, Lilly," he says with more seriousness than I think Z's ever spoken anything.

"What's it about?"

"It's not some pretty accessory."

"I think that's pretty clear."

His voice takes on a more solemn tone. "Colors were picked long before I was a member."

"How'd you become a member?"

"How? I don't even know how to answer that."

"Would you answer it?"

He sighs and spreads his hands in front of him. "What do you want to know, Lilly?"

What am I doing? What am I trying to gain from this? "You'll answer my questions?"

He pulls away from me, sitting on the edge of his bed. "I'll answer what I can."

"Can women be members?"

An amused snort bursts out of him. "None have ever asked."

"What about Trinity?"

"She doesn't ride."

"Why not?"

"You'd have to ask her."

"But she's allowed to?"

"Ride? Shit, yeah. She can do whatever she wants."

"The big scary guy would let her?"

My question elicits a soft chuckle out of him. "Please make sure to call him that to his face."

"I'm serious."

"You worried about Trinity?" he asks in his short clipped way that somehow comes out soft and more happy that I care about Trinity than annoyed about my obnoxious questions. "Trin has a mind of her own. I'm sure if she wanted to ride she would," he finally says.

"What's the "property of" thing mean? Seems pretty caveman."

He rolls his eyes before answering. "It's too complicated to explain right now."

"You think I'm too stupid to get it?"

"No. I'm just not sure if you have an open mind. Hope has a patch too, you know."

That's interesting. Maybe I'll ask Hope about it instead since I don't think I'm going to get anywhere with Z.

"How come Trinity's vest doesn't have the skull and crown?"

This time, I get a lopsided grin. "She ain't a member. Colors are for members."

I'm out of questions.

"You done?" Z asks.

"I reserve the right to ask more questions later."

Reaching out a hand, he crooks his finger at me. "Come here, pretty girl."

I slip my shoes off, leaving them next to his dresser and make my way to him.

His big hands slide up my legs up under my dress until he's gripping my upper thighs. Not hard. Not to hurt. Just enough to drive me crazy. "What's with all the questions? You've never been interested in this stuff before."

I can't explain it. Maybe it's from hanging out with all

of his brothers tonight. As well as guys from other clubs. Before tonight, I'd only interacted with Hope's now-husband, Rock. I'd seen Trinity's man once or twice. And of course, Z. But tonight was different.

Now, I'm curious.

"I don't know. I realized, hanging out with so many of your brothers, it made me think, I don't know anything about that part of your life."

"You never wanted to."

"So, now I do."

His features turn serious. Serious Z is a little intimidating. "Why?"

"I don't know."

"Is it general curiosity? Or do you want to know *me* better?"

Now, *that's* a loaded question.

Zero

I need to know the answer to my question, but not for the reason she probably thinks. Is she nosy for info about the club so she has some fun stories to tell her friends? Or does she honestly want to know more about *me*?

She seems to think over my question, which doesn't bother me. I like how thoughtful she is about something so important.

"I guess, seeing everyone tonight…I realized your club, it's more than a social thing."

I release my hold on her legs, and she backs up a few steps. "It's a brotherhood."

She shakes her head. "What does that mean?"

"It's about loyalty. We always have each other's backs. No matter what."

"I've only ever felt that way about family."

"They're my family."

"No, my brother—"

"I know what *you* meant. I'm explaining my outlook to you. They *are* my brothers." I tap my fist over my heart, so she gets it. "Doesn't matter if we share blood, I'd bleed for anyone of them, and they'd do the same for me." That's the truth, and it's even happened once or twice.

"Does that loyalty extend to the women?"

"Hope and Trinity? Fuck yeah, it does. Teller's sister, Heidi, too."

At the mention of Heidi's name, Lilly's lush mouth turns up in a smile. "She's such a nice kid."

"Yeah, don't let her fool you. She's a little badass. Doesn't need us protecting her as much as you'd think."

Lilly chuckles and I realize I'm having fun talking about this stuff with her. Happy she seems curious and more open-minded than I've given her credit for. I've always appreciated how loyal she is to Hope. Now, the way she seems concerned about Trinity and Heidi—fuck, I like that too. She'd probably rip my balls off for saying it out loud, but Lilly's good ol' lady material.

But I think we've come as far as we can with this conversation for tonight.

"Come back here."

I've been hard for Lilly all day, but the way she reacts to my no-room-for-argument tone, works me up even more. Her breathing kicks up. Short, quick breaths that make her chest rise and fall.

"Turn around."

She hesitates before turning. There's a rush that comes with telling a willful woman like Lilly to do something and watching her struggle between telling me to *fuck off* and doing it that's hot as fuck. My hands find their way to her smooth legs. Tracing my fingers behind her knees and up to the backs of her thighs makes her giggle softly.

"That tickles," she whispers. Laughter turns into a sharp moan when my hands find their way to her ass and squeeze. Perfect.

Reaching up, I drag the zipper of her dress down. "Take it off."

Her shoulders lift, letting the dress fall to the floor. Gracefully, she leans over and pulls the dress off her foot, tossing it on my desk.

I like the way Lilly holds herself—there's nothing about Lilly I don't like—but I admire her confidence. Straight spine, shoulders back. Her long hair almost reaches the small of her back

Standing, I wrap one arm around her waist and press her tight to me.

I drag my lips over her shoulder. "Admit we're good together, Lilly," I whisper as I kiss my way to her ear.

"So good."

The fact that she didn't bother with a bunch of half-hearted protests or a smart-ass comeback makes me say something else I wasn't planning on. "You know you're the last thing I think about before I go to sleep? The only face I picture when I close my eyes?" It's so much easier to tell her these things when she's not facing me.

"Me too," she whispers so low, I almost don't hear her.

Surprised she'd admit it, I squeeze her a little tighter. Her head falls forward. But one of her hands sneaks between us, closing around my dick, rubbing the hard length through my pants. I groan, jerking my hips forward.

"You want that?"

"Yes."

"Do you think you deserve it?"

She snorts. "Probably not."

I add my rumbling chuckles to her softer laughter. "Think you can take it?"

"Oh, I know I can."

I move my hand up, cupping her breast and grazing my thumb over her nipple. Against my body she shivers.

"Z," she says on a ragged exhale of breath. "Don't make me wait."

"Why not? You made me wait. Tortured me last night, knowing you were here and I couldn't have you."

"That's not fair." I can practically hear the pout in her voice.

"No, it wasn't."

Guiding her with my hands on her hips, I turn her to face me. She's tired of me messing with her, because she twists her fingers in my hair and pulls me to her for a rough kiss. She crushes my mouth against hers, but that's where I take over. I brush my fingers through her hair, wrapping it tight around my fist and give her a gentle tug. It's enough to make her pause so I can slide my tongue inside her mouth. She breathes a soft moan into me and kisses me back so hard I groan. My lips slide down her jaw to her throat, and she arches her back, pressing herself into me.

I pull away and grip her exploring hands. "Get my dick out." I slip off my shirt and it lands somewhere on the floor. I'm not real worried about it. No, all I can think about is her hands quickly working my pants open, pushing everything down to free my aching dick. A soft hiss of air eases out of me as she takes me in both of her soft hands.

"What do you want?"

Instead of answering, she lowers herself to the floor in front of me. My eyes zero in on her tongue as she runs it over her lips. I'm dying to get inside her, but I'm also having fun teasing her. Gently, I press my hand to her forehead, pushing her back.

"Stay still. I'll let you know when you can have it."

She flicks her eyes up at me in surprise and probably annoyance. I give her a second, and she sits back, waiting for what happens next.

"Open."

The second her lips slide over the head of my cock, my legs hum with pleasure. The sensation travels up my spine. Pleasure leaves me groaning as her warm, wet mouth surrounds me. She swirls her tongue around me, then sucks greedily.

"Good girl."

I get another pissy look for that one, but it only gets me harder.

"Take it all, Lilly."

She takes me right to the back of her throat over and over, never backing off until I hold her head still. "Up."

Lilly

ONLY SLIGHTLY ANNOYED, I kiss my way up Z's body. When I'm standing, he brings his mouth near mine, hovering for a second. I want him to kiss me more than anything.

And he does. He grabs the back of my head and kisses fiercely. I open for him because there's no point denying how much I want him.

I push, but Z's a mountain of man and muscle. Impossible to move.

"What do you want, Lilly?" he asks.

"You."

His lips curve, and there's a hint of arrogance in his eyes that makes me want to smack him. Then he drops his gaze, uses his thumbs to roughly pull my bra down. Frustrated because the material refuses to cooperate, he reaches around and unhooks it, flinging it away. One roughened hand cups my breast the other one dips lower. He holds my gaze as he slides two fingers between my legs. They slip into place easily because I've been ready for him all day.

I'm not prepared for the intense look in his eyes when he spins me around, pushing me onto his bed. The noise in my head goes silent under the weight of his stare. He climbs on the bed after me, kicking his pants and shoes off. "Come here, pretty girl." His raspy voice pulses through my body, filling me with desire.

The crinkle of a wrapper draws my attention from his eyes. I watch him slide into a condom. He eases my knees apart, opening me.

"Yeah, this is what I've been waiting for, all fucking day," he says, closing the distance between us. He circles and taps my clit with his cock. Teasing me again. How the hell can he stand it?

"Will you fuck me already?"

My demand finally snaps his iron control, and he pushes into me. Z's a lot to handle, but I love every bit of his thick length inside me.

He groans and halts his movements. "Fuck. You're tight as hell. Miss me?"

"Yes," I whisper because I'm tired of playing hard to get with him. Uncomfortable being so open, I bury my face in his neck. He takes mercy on me and works his hips, each thrust slow, hard and deliberate.

"Give me your mouth, Lilly."

Shaking my head, I nip at the muscles of his shoulder. "Careful. I might bite back."

I can't help it, though. His massive frame is such a turn-on. I've never been with another man who's such a solid wall of muscle. Who knows how to use all those muscles to please me in every way.

"Lilly," he warns.

I roll my hips up to meet him and he groans. "Fuck. So fucking good," he mutters. His pace slows to a lazy grind and one of his hands grips my chin, turning my face, kissing my lips.

He forces his tongue into my mouth at the same time he drives into my pussy hard and relentless. The dual assault leaves me panting. I raise my legs, wrapping them around his waist.

"Good girl," he praises, slipping a hand under my ass,

angling me up even more.

If he wasn't balls deep inside me, I'd smack him for that *good girl* comment. But all I care about are his primal grunts and punishing thrusts.

Every muscle in my body tightens around him, and Z slows, not wanting me to come so quick. But it's too late. I gasp and arch my back and get carried away by a sweeping orgasm.

Zero

MAYBE IT'S the wedding that has her so hot. She claimed not to be the marrying kind, but she's wilder than she's ever been before.

And Lilly is pretty fucking wild.

When she opens her eyes, I slide out of her and urge her onto her hands and knees, thrusting back inside before she's fully ready for me.

"Fuck!" she yells out, and I grunt in agreement. My arm bands tight around her waist pulling her against me at the same time as I plow into her. It's hotter. Heat's just pouring off her. Slicker.

So fucking amazing.

Every little flutter, every muscle tightening around my dick rockets through me. Why aren't we doing this all the time? Why am I waiting for her to figure her shit out instead of telling her how it's going to be? We're fucking amazing together. And if she'd let us, we could be more than fantastic fucking sex.

"Lilly," I groan her name through my release. My

entire body stills, tightens, pouring everything I have into her.

I pull in a few shaky breaths before sliding out of her and staggering off the bed. She collapses into a cute little puddle, all plush ass in the air, perfectly thick thighs, unblemished skin and sex-mussed hair.

Something wet hits my foot, and I glance down.

My dick's poking out of the condom, cum leaking everywhere.

"Fuck," I mutter. "Lilly?"

"*Mmm?*" She rolls over and I swear my dick's already getting hard again from just the sight of her fantastic tits.

I point down. "Condom broke. I'm sorry I didn't realize it sooner."

Anger? Horror? Shock? I'm not sure. Maybe a mix of those three emotions flicker over her face. "I'm clean, babe." Oh, I hate like fucking hell admitting this next part. "You're the only one I've—"

She has the nerve to roll her eyes. "I'm supposed to believe that?"

"Believe whatever you want." I stalk into the bathroom and just barely stop myself from slamming the door. I take a few seconds to clean up and calm the fuck down. No one twists me up the way she does. *No one.*

When I emerge, a little more rational, she's sitting in the bed with her knees drawn up, the sheet covering her right to her chin.

"I'm sorry," she says softly. "You're the only...don't worry. I haven't been with anyone else in a long time. We're good."

Any lingering anger disappears, and I pounce on the

bed, ripping the sheet away from her and replacing it with my body. "Really?" I ask, drawing the word out until I get her to laugh.

"Yeah, really. Don't be so smug." She reaches out and cups my cheek, her soft fingers brushing against my skin. "I think you've ruined me for any other man."

"Nothing wrong with that." I move in closer for a kiss and she makes this little noise that sounds like either agreement—

Or denial.

I COULD GET USED to waking up with Lilly next to me.

Even after the broken condom fiasco.

She makes me think about all sorts of things I never considered before meeting her.

But Lilly's a tricky one. I try to talk to her about us moving from fuck buddies to serious couple, she shuts me down.

Every fucking time.

It's annoying. And if she wasn't the hottest fuck I've ever had as well as the smartest chick I've ever spent time with, I would have lost her number long time ago.

Soft scratching at my bedroom door pulls me out of bed. The pups wriggle and dance their way into the room. After being displaced last night, it was a miracle they hadn't howled or scratched at my door all night. "Uncle Sparky take care of you?" I whisper as I bend down to scratch behind their ears. "I owe you two extra cookies."

I throw a quick glance at Lilly—still sound asleep and

slip on a pair of sweats before running the dogs downstairs and outside.

A few guys are still up. Stash and Ravage are busy smoking dope in the living room. Dex is there too but seems to be halfway sober. Swan's sort of passed out in his lap. I lift my chin at her. "She okay?"

"Yeah," he answers slowly.

"You should have seen the show she put on in the champagne room last night," Ravage says, wiggling his eyebrows or emphasis and earning a scowl from Dex.

Great. Always has to be some complication around here.

"Where's Willow? She go home?" I ask.

Stash raises his eyebrows and points to the basement door. "With Sparky."

"Really?" Man, I can't wait to rib Willow this week at the club.

Stash shrugs, but there's a lingering smirk that makes me want to press him for details.

"Oh my God, why are you guys up at this hour?" Trinity asks from the hallway. I turn and find her dressed to work out, an inexplicable smile stretched across her face.

"What are you doing up so early? Shouldn't you be exhausted from your maid of honor duties? Or from your man?" Ravage asks.

"Watch it," Wrath growls coming up behind her and yanking her against him. He leans down, whispering something in her ear that makes her laugh softly and smack his chest. Without saying anything else, she turns and heads back down the hall.

"Why so grumpy?" I ask.

Wrath grins. "Oh, I ain't grumpy at all."

Intrigued, Ravage and Stash sit up. "What's up, bro?" Ravage asks.

"Nothing. Later."

With those cryptic words, Wrath turns and walks down the hall.

"Something's up with those two," Ravage says.

"Wow. You could be like a detective or something," Stash snarks at him before lighting another joint and inhaling deep.

"Fuck off."

"This has been fun, but I've got a hot, naked chick in my bed."

"Need some help with that?" Stash asks, just to be a dick.

"No, ya fuck," I growl at him.

The two fuckwits have a good laugh. Dex just rolls his eyes. The pups jump up on the couch and settle into the cushions behind Swan.

"Watch them?" I ask.

"Yeah. No problem," Ravage answers.

I take the stairs two at a time and let out a breath when I find Lilly still sound asleep.

Fuck I like having her here.

I slip into bed next to her and watch as she slowly wakes.

"Morning."

She gives me an uncertain look before stretching.

"How long have you been up?" she asks in her sexy-morning-husky voice.

"Few minutes. Had to run the dogs out."

She picks her head up and looks around. "Where are they?"

"Downstairs."

"Sorry. You didn't have to kick them out because of me. I like dogs."

In a sweet gesture that I don't think she gives much thought to, she leans in and kisses my forehead before tossing the covers back. I admire her naked ass all the way to the bathroom and wait for her to come back.

She returns wearing one of my T-shirts.

"I can't vouch for how clean that is if you picked it up off the bathroom floor," I warn her.

Her nose wrinkles and she pulls at the shirt to smell it. "It smells good. Like you."

She jumps on the bed and crawls back under the covers, snuggling up to me.

This is nice.

Real nice. I could totally get used to this.

Maybe it's time to stop fucking around and be straight with her. No more jokes or half-ass attempts. Real shit.

And when she says no, I'll fuck her until she says yes.

Lilly

I hate how much I liked waking up in Z's arms. I like my independence. Sleeping in my own bed. Not having to worry about impressing someone twenty-four-seven.

But I really like Z. I'm comfortable around him. Something I never expected.

He's so warm and hard against me, I wriggle, trying to

get closer. Not because I'm cold, but because I like how he feels. How *this* feels.

Tipping my head back, I catch him staring at me with an intensity I've never seen. Not sexual.

Something's on Z's mind. On the outside he seems calm, but I see his pulse at his neck fluttering. I reach over and place my hand over his heart. It's racing.

"What's on your mind, Z? You look like you're about to have a stroke."

He doesn't even crack a smile at my idiotic teasing.

"Last night. Remember how we both admitted we've only been seeing each other?"

"Uh, I don't think that's what we said." He keeps staring at me until I fidget. "We said we hadn't *fucked* anyone else besides each other."

"Same thing," he growls, clearly frustrated with me.

But it's a lie. I've dated a bunch of guys in between seeing Z. I just haven't wanted to sleep with a single one. None of them. Try as I might to find someone else, my lady bits were on strike when it came to anyone other than this intense, sexy beast of a man.

"How about we officially only see each other." He doesn't really phrase it as a question. His voice never wavers and his eyes never leave my face, but he's so strained. So serious. And I have the feeling it's killing him not to declare I'm his like a caveman.

"You want me to be your girlfriend, Z?" I ask, just so I know we're both on the same page.

"I'm a little old for girlfriends, Lilly." He closes his eyes and when he opens them he's staring somewhere over my shoulder. "But we can start there if that's easier for you."

Wow. I don't know what else to think. My mind keeps repeating *wowwowowow*. "How does that look? You work in a strip club. You live here. Have girls around just to service you when you're feeling randy. You're on the road a lot. How…?"

The hardening of his expression makes me lose track of my own words.

"You never said anything about Crystal Ball before," he finally says.

"You never wanted to be a couple before."

"Bullshit," he mutters.

"I didn't say *no*. I'm asking questions."

"Fine. You want me to quit my job?"

Shit, do I? It seems unfair. I probably get hit on more often working at the legislature than he does in a strip club.

"No. That's not fair. Either I trust you or I don't."

He turns then, surprise written all over his face. Guess he didn't expect that answer.

"You want me to move out of the clubhouse?"

"Don't you *have* to live here?"

"No. Some of the guys live off-campus," he says with a smirk, as if I'd spoken my frat-house comment out loud last night.

"But you're happy here."

He doesn't say anything. Doesn't have to. I saw with my own eyes last night how at ease he is here. How much he likes being around the guys he considers his family.

"If anyone should move, it's me. You're here. My job's down in Empire…the commute—"

"I come before your job. That's a start," he says dryly.

There's a lot of noise, shouting and banging around in the hallway. Nothing alarming. Just the guys waking up and being guys. Z grinds his teeth as if it's bad timing, but I stop him with a hand on his shoulder.

"In the past, I've had interest from rental agencies...to rent my house out in the summers because it's so close to the lake. I could...I could rent an apartment closer to you." My heart's thumping so hard I barely get the words out.

He flicks his gaze my way and a brief smile touches his lips. "We can talk more about this later."

A breath of relief leaves me. Z's sensitive to my mood. He realizes how hard this is for me and he's giving me space.

"Let's go down for breakfast. I bet the happy couple will be over soon."

"Oh, good. I'd like to see Hope before I leave."

His mouth twists.

"How long do you want me to stick around?"

"I probably shouldn't answer that." He throws the covers off and in a fluid, sexy motion, pushes himself over top of me, caging me in with his thick, muscled arms. Not even a tremor from holding himself up over me. He dips down and kisses my forehead before moving off the bed.

"You're awfully graceful for such a big guy."

He smirks at me.

"Shit. My bag is down in Trinity's room. I don't have anything to wear besides my bridesmaid dress."

He doesn't tease me or hesitate. "I'll go grab it for you."

Maybe he's good for me after all.

Zero

I GOT FURTHER than I ever expected to with Lilly today. I'm not stupid, though. Sensing it was time to back off, I did. Her mind's turning, working it out in her head. That's enough for now.

Opening the door to run downstairs and grab her stuff, I almost trip over the bags in front of my door. I pick them up and turn to Lilly. "Yours?"

She lets out a soft laugh and nods.

Fifteen minutes later, we're headed into the dining room hand in hand. Trinity's at the usual table flipping through a big pink binder. "Christ, Trin, the wedding's over. Put that thing away."

Startled, she glances up and slams the binder closed, sliding it under her chair. "Morning."

"Where's your other half?" I ask as we approach the table. Lilly lets me pull a chair out for her and she even sits in it without a single comment.

Trinity points to the doorway, and I turn to see Wrath trying to sneak up on me. "Not today, fucker," I holler, dropping into the chair next to Lilly before he bear hugs me or whatever the fuck else he was planning to do.

He's wearing the same shit-eating grin he had on earlier. "What's up, brother?"

He falls into the chair next to Trinity and flings an arm around her shoulders. "I'll tell you in a few."

Now I'm really curious. But he turns his head, nuzzling against Trinity's shoulder and whispering something in her ear that makes her laugh.

After a few minutes she glances around the dining room. "I'll go check on the girls—"

Wrath clamps his hand over her leg, keeping her in place. "Not today," he says, just loud enough for me to hear it.

Lilly catches my eye and I shrug.

Murphy and Teller join us next. Teller looks worn out while, Murphy, I'm not sure what's going on with him. His knuckles on his right hand are scraped up, though. "Get into it last night, little brother?"

For some reason, he and Trinity share a look. "I'll tell you later."

"What the fuck is everyone so secretive for this morning?" I grouch.

Teller bursts out laughing. "Probably waiting for Mom and Dad to get here."

Wrath rolls his eyes. "Christ, they'll both kill you if they hear that."

Lilly shakes against me. "Mom and Dad?"

Murphy makes a circular motion with his hand, indicating everyone at the table. "Rock is the dad—"

"No, no, I get it." Lilly laughs even harder. "No wonder Hope doesn't want kids. She already has a house full of them."

Trinity laughs with her. "Exactly."

Serena and Mariella burst out of the kitchen with mugs and pour coffee for everyone. Lilly gives me a curious look but doesn't say anything.

"Hey, newlyweds!" Murphy shouts, making all of us turn our heads. Rock sort of glares at each of us and tries to tug Hope back out the door.

"How was the wedding night?" Wrath yells.

I can't resist messing with them either. "Was it worth saving yourself for?" I ask.

Prez rolls his eyes and glances at Hope. "I told you we should have eaten breakfast at home."

She shushes him and they take their seats. Hope's a sharp girl. She looks around the table, taking each of us in. She smiles briefly when she notices Lilly's still here. But her gaze goes back to Wrath and Trinity who have matching grins stretched across their faces.

"What's up with you two?" she asks.

Right before she says it, I catch Wrath's eye and he looks so fuckin' happy I know exactly what Trinity's about to say. "We're engaged!"

The girls shriek and Hope races over to see the ring. Lilly joins them and they chatter away. I stand, reaching over to give Wrath a quick hug and back slap. "Congratulations, brother."

I *could* make some ball and chain joke, but I'm too happy for the both of them.

"I am *not* going to any dress shops," Murphy informs all of us. Yeah, that had been fun. For Wrath and me, *not* Murphy. I eye Wrath because we need to make Murphy do that again, but he's too busy staring at his bride-to-be.

Then they're busy making out and making everyone want to hurl. Lilly grins at me and leans over to kiss my cheek. "They're sweet together," she whispers.

"He'd do anything for her." I want her to understand, if she let me, I'd be just as devoted to her. I just can't come up with the right words.

Instead, I tease Rock and Hope about all the boring,

married sex they'll be having. Teller rats me out for the time or two I said Hope was dick-whipped.

Murphy finally explains why his knuckles are so raw. "I knocked Bull's ass out last night."

I'm sure Bull had that punch coming. Fuck, I wanted to punch him myself last night a few times. Lilly looks a little disgusted, so I shrug. This is who we are. If I want to get serious with her, she might as well hear it all, good and bad.

Serena and Mariella bring out a platter of eggs, bacon, sausage, and toast, which we all demolish.

Wrath informs us he's planning to build a house next. I catch Lilly's eye. *See? I wouldn't expect you to live at the clubhouse,* I want to tell her.

Hope teases us, claiming she got a tattoo that Rock absolutely will not allow her to show us. Lilly leans in. "It must be true love. She always swore she'd never get a tattoo."

"Yeah, what about you?"

She raises an eyebrow. "I've never had something I wanted on my body permanently."

"I wanna be on your body permanently," I growl in her ear. She shivers and turns to catch my mouth in a quick kiss.

"For fuck's sake. Y'all need to get a room!" Dex shouts. He's not yelling at me specifically. Rock and Hope barely glance up at Dex's bitching. Wrath throws his middle finger up without taking his mouth off Trinity.

"Thank fuck," Teller groans, pulling out a chair for Dex. "I'm about to lose my breakfast."

Mariella pokes him in the side, and he grins at her.

Murphy's sitting next to Serena looking like he's choking on a piece of bark. "You okay, lil' brother?"

"I'm good."

"Did Heidi come back last night?" Hope asks Teller who groans.

"No. She called me when he dropped her off, though." He glances over at the bar at the few people snoring on top of it. "Too much going on here last night, you know?"

She laughs. "I see your point."

Rock claps his hands once to get our attention. "Church. Then my bride and I are going to pack for Hawaii."

"Are you *letting* her bring clothes, Rock?" Trinity asks, bursting into giggles.

Rock's mouth twists into a wicked smirk, but he doesn't answer.

"Thanks, Trin," Hope mutters. She's laughing too, though.

Rock glances at me but before he says anything, Murphy stands. "I'm gonna walk Serena out and then I'll round the guys up for church."

I think it's news to Serena that she's leaving.

"Thanks for all your help, Serena," Mariella calls out.

Serena nods and follows Murphy.

After they clear the dining room, Trinity jumps up. "While you guys are in church, I *am* helping Mariella clean up," she says with a pointed look at Wrath, who rolls his eyes. Hope joins her before Rock can say no.

"I feel like I should help now too," Lilly jokes.

I lean into her. "We won't be long. Will you still be here?"

She turns and presses a quick kiss to my lips. Her fingers trail over my cheek and she looks into my eyes. "I'll stick around."

Z and Lilly's trilogy starts with Zero Tolerance.

THE LOST KINGS MC SERIES

STAND ALONES IN THE LOST KINGS WORLD
Bullets & Bonfires
Murphy and Teller appear here.
Warnings & Wildfires
Wrath and Murphy appear here.
Cards of Love: Knight of Swords
Dex and Murphy appear here.

ABOUT THE AUTHOR

Autumn Jones Lake is the *USA Today* and *Wall Street Journal* bestselling author of over twenty novels, including the popular Lost Kings MC series. She believes true love stories never end.

Her past lives include baking cookies, bagging groceries, selling cheap shoes, and practicing law. Playing with her imaginary friends all day is by far her favorite job yet!

Autumn lives in upstate New York with her own alpha hero.

www.autumnjoneslake.com